Clara in

Copyright © 2016 by Stacey Cartlidge
All rights reserved. This book or any portion thereof
may not be reproduced or used in any manner
whatsoever
without the express written permission of the
publisher
except for the use of brief quotations in a book review.

This is a work of fiction. Names, characters, places and incidents either are products of the author's imagination or are used fictitiously. Any resemblance to actual events or locales or persons, living or dead, is entirely coincidental.

For my husband.
I probably drove you insane whilst writing this book.
The least I could do was dedicate it to you.

Chapter 1

Flowers. We all love them. Whether it's a classic red rose, some pretty peonies or a bunch of striking sunflowers, there's a flower out there for all of us. If you'd have asked me a few months ago what my favourite flower was, I would probably have said roses. Not because I felt strongly about roses, but because I didn't really have a clue about any others. Now, looking around the florist's that has become my second home, I have fallen in love with so many. Gerberas, lilies, daffodils, tulips...

'*Carnations?*' Believe me, no woman wants to receive *carnations* on their birthday!' Janie lets out a scoff and boldly leans over the counter, narrowly avoiding an awkward wardrobe malfunction. 'How about orchids? Can you afford orchids?' She takes the wallet out of the customer's hands as he stares at her in bewilderment. 'Let's see, how much have you got in here?'

I smile apologetically at the poor man who now looks frozen to the spot. That bloody woman should come with a warning! We're not going to have any customers left at this rate. Shaking my head at my outspoken mother-in-law, I shoot her a glare and get back to arranging a vase of purple freesias. Sensing my annoyance, Janie exhales loudly and begrudgingly stands up straight.

'Fine.' She attempts a small smile, but her disdain at his choice of flowers is clear to see. 'Carnations it is...'

After applying a layer of red gloss to her collagen filled lips, she begrudgingly wraps a selection of the pink flowers in delicate tissue paper. In a matter of seconds, her wrinkly fingers twist the stems together, creating a beautiful bespoke bouquet. Watching her take the cash and slam the till shut with her hip, I wait until the customer has left the building before turning to face her.

'OK, you *have* to stop doing that.' I give her a stern look and fold my arms, trying my hardest not to lose my temper.

'What?' Janie's Texan drawl echoes around the room and I rub my throbbing temples.

'If people want carnations, just give them carnations.' Taking the vase of freesias and placing it at the front of the window display, I flip the sign over to *closed* and lean against the door.

'Would *you* want carnations?' She attempts to raise an already terrifyingly high eyebrow and grins smugly.

Dammit. I certainly would not want to receive carnations. Knowing that she's got me over a barrel, I bite my lip and look out of the window. Carnations have always reminded me of a tacky apology from a guilty man. You know the kind, a lame gift picked up from the petrol station in a last-ditch attempt at salvaging a failing relationship. Not that I admit this to the customers, obviously.

'I... I don't mind carnations.' I say this confidently, secretly knowing that she's aware I absolutely *hate* carnations.

Janie looks at me suspiciously for a moment before finally tearing her eyes away unconvinced. She knows that I'm lying, but I really don't care. What I *do* care about is her scaring away our customers with her outspoken and opinionated ways. It's not like this is the first time it's happened either. After three months of sporadic shifts and numerous disgruntled clients, her customer service skills haven't improved one iota. I think we can safely say that public relations are *not* her strong point. To be honest, I really shouldn't be surprised. I mean, my mother-in-law doesn't exactly have a reputation for being a people person. I have lost count of the number of times I've had to apologise for Janie's outrageous behaviour, and I don't just mean here at the florist's.

Checking over the remaining stock, I discard the last of the withered flowers into the recycling bin and flip the lid shut. This is my least favourite part of the job. Throwing away beautiful flowers just because they have turned a little brown around the edges makes me feel rather sad. When the florist's first opened, we used to take the leftover stock to the retirement home across town, but due to new health regulations and a rather pedantic district manager, we were told they would no longer be able to accept them. Pretty stupid if you ask me. I did try taking them home to make potpourri, but Oliver soon put a stop to that when he mistook them for crisps as he looked for a midnight snack.

Stacking the recycling bins together, I scan the room for anything that I might have missed and place them neatly by the back door. Poor flowers. I have a sneaky feeling that the eccentric bohemian lady from across the street slips them into her shopping cart before the containers are collected. I look out of the window and spot her tying an array of plastic bags to the handles on her trolley. Every single day she sits in the same spot, wearing the same outfit and shouting the same curse words. I've never spoken to her, but for some reason, I feel like I know her. Her familiar wiry hair and crazy clothes have become a permanent fixture for us here on Teller Street. Don't ask me why, but seeing her sitting there come rain or shine makes me feel strangely safe and watching her shout at the snooty bankers as they step over her has made us laugh on many occasions.

Janie swears under her breath, bringing me out of my daydream with a thud. Spinning around, I watch her rubbing furiously at the green stains on her skirt, making the messy marks ten times worse.

'Damn flowers. This is the third outfit I've ruined this week!' Shaking her head, she says some words that I wouldn't want to repeat and sighs dramatically.

'I don't know why you won't just wear an apron like the rest of us.' Tearing off my own apron, I shake down the lilac canvas and place it on its hanger.

'Please, do I look like the kind of woman who wears *aprons?*' She throws back her head and laughs like a crazy person.

Looking her up and down, I have to admit that she certainly does not look like the kind of woman who wears aprons. Poured into a pink pencil skirt and a shockingly low-cut blouse, she doesn't exactly look like the kind of woman who works in a florist's either. Well, Janie doesn't technically *work* here, but due to an unexpected emergency, she offered to step in and give me a helping hand. I guess I shouldn't really be complaining, Janie has had to come to our rescue on more than one occasion lately.

When my good friend and owner of the florist's, Eve, realised she had miscalculated her dates and that she was ovulating today, she threw down her apron and practically ran out of the shop, leaving just myself and my co-worker, Dawn, to cope with the lunchtime rush. Before I could have a complete meltdown, Janie stepped up to the plate and saved the day. Even though she drives me completely insane, without her help we would have had a hundred unhappy customers today, rather than just the two that she has managed to upset on her own.

If you haven't already guessed, I'll let you in on a secret. Eve and her husband, Owen, are trying for a baby. Well, I call it a secret, but everyone who is anyone knows that the Lakes have been longing for a child for a good couple of years now. I still find it hard to believe that the once child-phobic Eve wants to become a mother. Eve Lake, the same woman who declared that she didn't *ever* intend on having kids and used whatever mothering instincts she had on a pack of spoilt Pomeranians. A smile plays on my lips as I picture my gorgeous and immaculate friend in my mind. Blonde hair, blue eyes and a body fat percentage to rival most athletes. There's no denying that she would most definitely be the yummiest of mummies.

It was on a trip to Barbados a couple of years back that Eve's biological clock finally started to tick. At the time, we put her sudden change of heart down to one too many rum punches and perhaps a little heat stroke, but she has been obsessed with the idea ever since. Even Owen, who at first was completely against the idea, has been hit with a serious case of baby fever. Just last week he randomly called by the apartment to take Noah to the park. Between me and you, I think Owen is trying to get some practice under his belt before he hears the pitter-patter of tiny feet for himself. It's ridiculously cute, watching the two of them walk off together, laughing and joking like a pair of teenagers even though there are more than forty years between them.

Unfortunately for the Lakes, all their baby-making hasn't been very productive and after twenty-four months of regulated sex sessions, they are still minus a child. Eve's inability to conceive is actually why she ended up owning this place, Floral Fizz. Understandably, she was getting rather downtrodden with the whole baby situation and we were starting to get a little worried about her. Various therapy sessions proved to be useless and counselling didn't seem to be working, so Owen thought buying Eve a business of her own would help to take her mind off things. At first, I was a little sceptical. I mean, how does giving someone a company stop them from being broody? Although I have to hand it to Owen, having Floral Fizz really has worked wonders on lifting Eve's spirits.

In a matter of months, Eve has made this florist's into a baby of her own and there isn't a day that goes by where she isn't consumed with bouquets, petals or Champagne. I say Champagne, because in true Eve style, she managed to design a florist's that not only sells the most stunning flowers, but also has a specialist selection of some of the best Champagnes in the world. With Eve being the self-confessed queen of bling, I wouldn't expect anything less.

'Are we done for the day?' Dawn asks, poking her head out of the workshop and bursting my thought bubble.

Looking up, I let out a laugh as I take in Dawn's flustered appearance. With foliage in her tousled hair, a dozen sticky labels on her t-shirt and soil on her nose, it's fair to say that she looks a little frazzled, to say the least.

'We most certainly are.' I reach over and pull a small branch out of her hair and toss it into the bin.

'Thank God!' Dawn lets out a dramatic sigh of relief and leans against the counter.

Bless her, she really is a trouper. There's not a day that goes by where she doesn't put a hundred and ten percent into her work. I still remember the day that Eve hired Dawn. After tons of terrible interviews and a few failed background checks, Eve had begun to give up hope of ever finding the perfect candidate. Then one day, the stars aligned and a chance meeting in a local coffee shop brought the two of them together. Whilst fumbling with her handbag at the till, Eve managed to spill the entire contents of her purse onto the floor and had a breakdown right there in the middle of the café.

Ever the good Samaritan, Dawn jumped to her feet and rushed to Eve's rescue. The two of them got to talking and Eve offered Dawn the job on the spot. It turned out that Dawn had quit her job the week prior after a fortune teller told her she would find her dream job in seven hours, seven days, seven weeks or seven years. Accurate, I know. When Eve mentioned she was struggling to find a florist, Dawn saw this as the green light she was waiting for and signed on the dotted line that very day. In true fairy-tale style, Dawn was welcomed into the Floral Fizz family and we have never looked back.

'Before I forget, I'm not going to be here tomorrow, so I've left the bridal collection for the Logan wedding in the storeroom.' Dawn wipes her hands on her apron and lets out a lion worthy yawn.

'Got it.' Nodding in response, I grab a cloth and start to wipe down the messy work surfaces. 'I'm leaving at midday, but Janie will be here.'

Dawn's eyes widen as she gives Janie a dubious glance. 'OK...' She says slowly, looking between Janie and I with a look of horror on her face.

'It will be *fine.*' I place a reassuring hand on her arm, but Dawn just purses her lips and heads over to the wash station.

It's safe to say that Dawn and Janie don't really see eye to eye. With Dawn being a self-proclaimed perfectionist, who will spend hour upon hour making sure that not a single petal is out of place, she cannot stand Janie's slapdash attitude to her work. I guess you could say that Dawn is high-maintenance, slightly obsessive and perhaps a little anal, but she is damn good at her job. I don't think I've ever met someone with the creative flair and passion that she has. Whilst the rest of us buzz around the shop floor like headless chickens, Dawn locks herself in the workshop and loses herself in a mountain of pollen and perfume. She really is Floral Fizz's prized asset and we would be completely lost without her.

Unlike Dawn, I wasn't born with the skills to transform a bunch of flowers into a spectacular display of colour and vibrancy. I can, however, be trusted to serve customers without offending them, whereas my delightful mother-in-law cannot. It would be an understatement to say that Janie and I have had somewhat of a turbulent relationship over the years. I know that most people complain about their mother-in-law, but mine really does take the biscuit. For those of you who don't know, Janie divorced her husband and moved to the UK around six months ago. Their forty-year marriage was dissolved in just sixty days and Janie has been living in our spare room ever since.

Ever the exhibitionist, Janie announced that she was leaving Randy on a surprise trip to Orlando for my son's birthday. Once the initial shock had worn off, I foolishly allowed myself to relax, only for Oliver to drop the life-changing bombshell on me that would lead us to where we are today. I knew at the time that it was a terrible idea, but how do you say *no* to your husband when he asks if his crying mother can come and live with you? Oliver swore that it would just be a temporary measure, that she would be on a flight back to America in no time at all. Unfortunately, after twenty-four long, tiring and incredibly frustrating weeks, Janie is still very much with us.

I know it sounds horrible, but Janie is honestly the hardest person to live with in the entire world. Honestly, I think I would rather share a house with a pack of stray dogs. Let's face it, they would probably have better manners. From stealing my beauty products to never doing laundry and even bringing random men back to the apartment. Yes, you heard me. My sixty-something mother-in-law actually brings booty calls back to the same apartment where her son and grandson are sleeping. You might be thinking that I am being quite blasé about this, but over the years I have become used to Janie's outlandish antics. Seriously, the stories I could tell you would have you squirming in your seat, but there's a time and a place for tales like that and now is not it.

'What's for dinner?' Janie asks, checking out her ludicrously long talons and groaning when she spots a minuscule chip.

I rack my brains in a poor attempt at recalling the contents of our practically bare fridge. We both know that I should have paid a trip to Waitrose yesterday and we also both know that I spent the entire evening watching re-runs of Tom and Jerry with Noah.

'I have no idea.' Checking my watch, I realise that I have just thirty minutes before Oliver gets home. 'I guess we will just have to grab something on the way back.'

'Well, it better be healthy.' Janie turns around and checks out her backside in the mirror. 'I swear my ass has *doubled* in size with all the crap that you eat.'

I flash her a glare and bite my lip in a bid to stop myself from saying something I will later regret. She has some nerve! In almost two hundred days, Janie hasn't offered to make dinner once. What she *has* done is complain about the number of calories in just about everything that we have eaten.

'Well, if you don't like what we're having you can always take yourself out for dinner...' Dumping the takings in the safe, I flick off the light and make a grab for my handbag.

'You trying to get rid of me, lady?' Janie adjusts the strap on her stripper style sandals and roughly shoves me out of the door.

Not bothering to respond, I zip up my jacket and wait for Dawn to gather her belongings. The busy street is cast in shadows from the many high buildings that line the roadside, providing a welcome relief from the strong sunshine that is peeking out from behind the clouds. Hordes of people dash along the pavement, each one seeming busier than the last, just itching to get to their destination before the next person. Smartly dressed businessmen weave through the crowds of teenagers who are happily talking amongst themselves. Their chatter is muffled by the sound of their glossy carrier bags crinkling as they walk.

Tipping back my head and taking a deep inhale of breath, I allow the vibe of the city to wash over me. A lot of people hate the hustle and bustle of London, but it really is my favourite city in the world. It's the only place I've ever been where I feel completely free and where just about anything seems possible.

'Alright.' Pulling down the shutters on the shop front, Dawn hauls her handbag onto her shoulder and holds out her arms for a hug. 'I better get going.'

'Enjoy your day off and I'll see you on Friday.' I give her a quick squeeze and step to the side to let a group of schoolgirls pass. 'You are coming, aren't you?' I add, ensuring that I keep my voice down so Janie doesn't hear me.

Dawn looks at me blankly for a second before a dawning realisation appears on her face.

'Friday!' She suddenly exclaims, hitting herself on the head playfully. 'Of course! I can't wait!'

I look up at the sky and sigh as Janie lets out a wolf whistle at a passing builder. Shoving her hands into her pockets, Dawn gives me a subtle wink before disappearing into the crowd of people. Right now, Friday can't come fast enough...

Chapter 2

'What's happening Friday?' Janie asks, quickening her pace and trying to keep up with me.

Sh... sugar! My brain goes into panic mode as I try and fail to come up with something that she won't possibly want an invite to. A museum tour? A children's party? Think, Clara! Think! In the end, I decide to tell the truth, well almost.

'We... are... going to a book club.' I offer her a thin smile and dodge a busker who is singing a rather good rendition of *Valerie*. 'This week it's vintage classics. We're reading *Of Mice and Men*. Do you want to join us?'

'Mice and men?' She curls her lip into a sneer and frowns. 'Let me get this right, you're seriously asking me if I wanna spend my Friday night reading about *mice?*' Janie looks at me as though I have lost my mind and continues to clack her way along the street. 'I think I'll pass.'

Swallowing the laugh that is bubbling in my throat, I push my way into a pizzeria and motion for Janie to follow me.

'Clara!' The friendly server raises his hand in acknowledgement and grins widely. 'This must be the third time this week! We just can't get rid of you!'

He laughs heartily and I feel my cheeks colour up. Well, this is kind of embarrassing. Other customers turn to look at me and I attempt to hide behind my handbag. I think when the local fast food joint starts knowing your name, it's time to throw out the takeout menus.

'Hi...' I squint my eyes in a bid to jog my memory. What the hell is his name?

'Antonio.' He mumbles, literally reading my mind.

'*Antonio!*' I confirm confidently, as though I had known this piece of information all along. 'Of course! How are you?'

'I am very well.' His smile falters a little and I suddenly feel bad for forgetting his name. 'Do you want your usual?'

I nod in response, not wanting to acknowledge that I have a *usual* out loud. In case you're wondering, my usual consists of two large pizzas, a couple of cheesy fries and a token side salad. I don't really know why I bother with the salad. It never gets eaten and we always end up throwing it away a couple of days later. I guess it just makes me feel a little less guilty about the appalling amount of saturated fat I am about to consume. It probably sounds terrible, feeding my hubby and child a plateful of carbs and trans fats, but when I've been working all day, I would rather chop off my eyelashes than fire up the oven.

Handing over some notes, I take a seat in a plastic chair and try to calm my growling stomach. Between arranging the morning delivery and attempting to keep up with the afternoon rush, the most I've managed to eat is a very questionable Pot Noodle. During my time on this planet I've had many, many jobs, but being on my feet all day in Floral Fizz has to be the most demanding by far. My mind flits back to the days when I could spend a couple of hours enjoying a leisurely lunch in my role as a stay at home mum and I feel a pang of longing. Who would have thought that working with a load of pansies (pardon the pun) could be so physically draining?

Looking up from my seat, I let out a groan as I spot Janie flirting outrageously with the delivery man. Twirling a strand of parched blonde hair around her fingers, she seems totally oblivious to the fact that she's making a complete fool of herself. Unfortunately, the delivery driver doesn't seem to agree with me and is lapping up her every word like a thirsty puppy desperate for water. Practically drooling down his shirt, he bites his lip as Janie lets out a laugh which sets her inflated chest off jiggling. Oh, please! Shaking my head, I stand to my feet as Antonio places my order on the counter.

'Clara, you're ready to go.' Banging his hand on the pizza box, he adjusts his cap and passes me a receipt.

'Thank you so much!' I gush, struggling to balance the giant boxes.

'No problema!' He tosses a few dips into the plastic bag. 'See you next week!'

I smile thinly and grab Janie by the arm. Not wanting to leave her admirer so soon, she huffs and puffs for a while before scribbling down her phone number and following me outside.

As we march down the street, Janie's phone pings loudly. Rolling my eyes, I try not to be sick as she digs out the handset and beams at the screen. No doubt that's the delivery guy. A quick glance at her phone confirms my suspicions. Jeez, whatever happened to playing it cool?

'You can't bring any more men back to the apartment.' I say firmly, already knowing that this is exactly what she is planning on doing.

Janie slaps me on the back playfully and lets out a cackle. 'Will you relax? We were just talking! You really think I'm that easy?'

'Unfortunately for me, I *know* you are...'

It's safe to say that Janie has developed somewhat of a *type* since she split from Randy. It generally goes something like this... under thirty, painfully skinny and with such little women experience that they believe Janie to be a catch. How she can be so confident in talking to men less than half her age is beyond me. I honestly don't know how she does it, but men can't seem to resist her. Seriously, they are like moths to a flame. When she first separated from Randy, Janie had a short fling with an Orlando native called Paulie. That particular relationship was more down to the fact that she managed to convince him she was a filthy rich entrepreneur who spent her days whizzing around Beverly Hills in a yellow Lamborghini, but that's another story entirely.

'Maybe I'll go and meet him for a nightcap...' She muses, smacking her lips together loudly.

'I mean it, Janie. There's to be no more men at the apartment, it's not fair on Noah. And don't try to sneak him in once we've gone to bed, because I'll know.'

Attempting to cross the street, I jump back onto the pavement as a cab whizzes past, almost knocking me off my feet. Damn London cab drivers. Why do they think the Highway Code doesn't apply to them? Red, stop. Green, go. I mean, how hard can it be? Concentrating on giving the driver a deathly stare, I don't realise that the traffic has come to a standstill. Before I have the chance to put one foot in front of the other, a group of power-dressed women shove past me, causing my pizza boxes to topple to the ground. Well, isn't that just fabulous? Letting out a silent scream, I drop to my knees and try to avoid being trampled on by the steady stream of suits marching on regardless.

'Can you give me a hand here?' Roughly shoving my wild curls out of my face, I look up at Janie who has strategically placed herself two feet away, obviously not wanting to be associated with the pathetic woman scooping melted cheese off the road.

Pretending that she can't hear a single word I'm saying, she deliberately turns away and waits for me to get my act together. Is she for real? Who sees somebody struggling and deliberately ignores them? Resisting the urge to thump her on the nose, I take a deep breath and tuck my hair out of my face. Grabbing the now filthy pizza, I shove it back into the box and stomp over the road. I catch a couple of teenagers sniggering in my direction and try to keep my eyes fixed firmly ahead. Disposing of the ruined food into a nearby bin, I clutch on to the remaining box as though my life depends on it.

Choosing to pretend that Janie no longer exists, I look straight ahead and don't turn back until I reach our apartment block. Punching the passcode into the keypad, I throw open the heavy glass door and jab at the lift button with my elbow. Praying that the lift arrives before she can catch up, I tap on the side of the box impatiently. Unfortunately, it looks like my luck isn't going to change anytime soon.

'Seriously?' Janie laughs as she totters inside in her absurd stilettoes. 'You're about to eat your weight in pizza and you can't even be bothered to take the damn stairs?'

Feeling my blood begin to boil, I give Janie a look that could melt stone and defiantly hit the lift button again.

'OK, but that ass of yours ain't gonna tone itself...' Hitching up her already short skirt, she adjusts her bra and trundles up the staircase.

Before I can yell something that I won't be able to take back, the lift doors spring open and I throw myself inside. Checking out my reflection in the less-than-flattering mirror, I have to admit that my arse *is* a little larger of late. I guess all of those McDonald's meals I've been inhaling on my lunch breaks are finally starting to show. Sucking in my stomach, I make a mental note to renew my gym membership and roll my aching shoulders. I've never been one of those infuriating women who can eat what they want and not gain a pound. You know the kind, the ones who devour cheeseburgers for breakfast and still look like they've stepped out of a gym advert. Sadly, staying slim has always been a challenge for me. Unlike my best friend, Lianna, I only have to look at a burger box and my cellulite shudders. Annoyingly, Li can eat like a hungry horse and still make most supermodels feel envious. And I mean that literally.

You see, for those of you who don't know, Lianna runs a rather prestige beach bar in Barbados with her hunky husband, Vernon. The Hangout is frequented by a somewhat celebrity clientele, with many of its customers being famous for one thing or another. Just last week she sent me a string of Whatsapp messages showing her comparing abs with Kendall and Kylie. I tried not to feel envious as I ate nachos on the couch and compared my muffin top to that of an overweight hamster.

The lift doors ping open and a wave of annoyance washes over me as I notice that Janie has beaten me to the finish line. Dammit. Sixty years old and she can still clear ten flights of stairs in three minutes flat. I've got to hand it to her, she might be an absolute terror to live with, but she is in bloody good shape for a woman of her age. I have tried to say this to her before, but somehow, she managed to turn this compliment into one of the world's worst insults.

A loud woofing drifts into the hallway and I find my lips stretching into a smile. After we had Noah, I didn't think it was possible to love another living thing as much as I love my son, but our new dog, Pumpkin, comes a close second. Ever since I first moved in with Oliver all those years ago, I found myself dreaming of fluffy butts and wagging tails. Oliver has always been sceptical of the practicalities of having a dog in an apartment, so when he finally gave in, I couldn't believe my luck. We fell in love with Pumpkin the second that we laid eyes on her. In a strange twist of fate, Oliver and I got lost on a trip up to Chester and stumbled across an animal sanctuary. Agreeing to have a quick look, we took one glance at Pumpkin's golden fur and decided that we just *had* to have her. This time last year we didn't even know that she existed and already we couldn't imagine life without her.

'Gimmie that.' Snatching the pizza box right out of my hands, Janie holds it above her head like a waitress and knocks loudly on our door.

Within seconds the door swings open, and the little face that I know and love beams up at us.

'Yay!' Noah yells, throwing his arms in the air and jumping up and down. 'Dad, Gee-Gee brought pizza!'

Trying to control Pumpkin, he holds on to her pink collar and pulls her back.

'I sure did!' Sashaying inside, Janie twirls around the box and drops it onto the table with a flourish, making sure to shoot Pumpkin a look of disgust in the process.

Noah squeals hysterically and jumps up onto a chair, his face alight with glee as Janie flips open to the lid to reveal the cheesy goodness. Planting a kiss on his head of chocolate curls, I want to scream that it was in fact *me* who got the pizza and it was also *me* who was left to pick up the petrol stained fragments of the other pizza from the middle of the road.

Leaning down to stroke Pumpkin's soft fur, I resist the urge to scoop her up and bury my face in her pink belly. Her big brown eyes light up as she licks my hand frantically, her tail wagging like a high-speed windscreen wiper. How have I lived without her for so long?

'How's my beautiful wife?' Oliver whispers, smiling down at me and giving my shoulders a quick squeeze. His American accent is starting to get a cockney twang, which automatically brings a smile to my face. 'You look tired. Tough day?'

Dragging myself away from Pumpkin, I reach up to kiss Oliver's beard clad cheek and shake off my coat.

'You could say that.' I kick off my boots and attempt to twist my crazy curls off my face. 'How was Gina?'

He nods and takes his phone out of his pocket, frowning at the screen as he takes a seat at the table. 'She just had Noah today, so she was a lot calmer than last week.'

I nod knowingly and start to gather some plates. When I decided to start working in Floral Fizz, Oliver and I had a little (OK, a *lot*) of trouble finding a nanny. Janie flat out refused and we just couldn't bring ourselves to leave our pride and joy with a total stranger. Don't get me wrong, everyone we met with was absolutely lovely, some had even worked for royalty, but I still felt a little uneasy about trusting someone I didn't know with Noah. Between me and you, I can't even leave Noah with Oliver without worrying that he's either dropped him or left him at the supermarket.

To cut a long story short, our good friend, Gina Stroker, who lives in the apartment above ours with our other good friend, Marc, had the genius idea of setting up her own childcare company. At first, I was a little dubious, I mean let's face it, despite having three of her own children, Gina isn't exactly the most *maternal* person on the planet. When she and Marc announced they were having Madison, no one could believe it. After all, she was the one who swanned around the office in animal print mini dresses and enough red lipstick to make a Vegas drag act feel washed out. Surprisingly, apart from the odd meltdown here and there, Gina has done fantastically well and the convenience of having her right upstairs just can't be beaten.

Grabbing some bottles of water from the fridge, I let out a sigh and squeeze into my seat. Pumpkin scurries around my feet, wagging her tail in a desperate bid for a slice of pizza. She offers me her paw and licks my hand hopefully. If only everyone could be as delighted at the prospect of a bit of bread and cheese. Discreetly opening her drawer, I take a handful of dog treats and drop them in front of her. Not one to turn her nose up at the offer of food, she gobbles them down and looks up for more. Shaking my head, I give her a quick scratch behind the ears and tell her to lie down.

'You just got the one pizza?' Oliver frowns as he takes a slice and hands it over to Noah, who immediately takes a giant bite. 'You know there are four of us, right?'

'Yes, Oliver. I am very aware of just how many people there are here.' I glance at Janie and give her a discreet scowl. 'I had a little mishap on the way home, and unfortunately had to throw the other one away...'

'You had to throw it away?' He mumbles, clearly confused as to what catastrophic event could have caused me to lose half of our dinner. 'Well, I guess we will just have to make do with one then...'

I take a deep breath to calm down and reach across the table for some chips, narrowly avoiding knocking over the unopened salad bowl in the process. Janie catches my eye and looks at my plate of fried goodies before pointing at my bum.

'Do you want some?' I ask, trying to sound innocent as I hold the greasy box under her nose, already knowing that she's going to say *hell no*.

Janie dips a carrot stick into a mound of hummus and crunches loudly, not bothering to dignify me with a response. Dropping the chips onto the table, I look at Oliver and wonder how on earth he can be so oblivious to the obvious tension between Janie and I. To be fair, he's not the most observant man in the world, but the fact that we are around three weeks away from killing each other is clear for *anyone* to see.

When I agreed to Janie living with us, my biggest concern was how Oliver would cope being in such close proximity to his mother. It's no secret that they don't have the best relationship, but almost unbelievably they seem to have grown closer than ever. After a not so squeaky-clean childhood, Oliver is finally reconnecting with his mum and I really don't want to be the one who breaks up their new-found friendship.

The fact that they're now getting along famously has only added to the hostility between Janie and I. No matter how hard I try, I just can't bring myself to tell Oliver that his mother is driving me up the wall. At first, I told myself not to be selfish. After all, it was just a temporary solution and only a matter of time before we waved her back off to America. But as the days turned into weeks and the weeks turned into months, the subject of Janie leaving became harder and harder to talk about. It's like it became a taboo topic, something that we weren't able to mention without someone looking uncomfortable and squirming in their seat.

Feeling my blood pressure start to rise, I pluck a slice of pizza from the box and dunk it into a mound of barbecue sauce. As I chew away at the delicious stuffed crust, I make a promise to myself that I will tackle the issue of Janie sooner rather than later. Is she ever planning on leaving? Who knows! What I *do* know is that we can't go on like this for much longer. Something has got to give...

Chapter 3

'Noah, you *can't* wear that.' Looking him up and down, I shake my head and quickly fasten my watch onto my wrist. 'Go and find something else, please.'

A wave of confusion washes over his face and I suddenly feel a little bad. For the past few weeks, Noah has been choosing his own clothes and until recently he has been pretty much on the money. Today, however, is a different story entirely. Dressed in a Spiderman mask, last year's pirate Halloween costume and mismatched socks, he looks frankly ridiculous and certainly not nursery appropriate.

Watching him drop his head and begrudgingly make his way back to his bedroom, I rifle through my handbag to check for all the essentials. Pumpkin jumps to her feet and pads across the kitchen tiles, stopping to stretch out her legs as she goes. Opening the balcony doors, I give her a quick stroke and shoo her outside. The fact that our balcony is larger than most gardens is such a blessing when it comes to Pumpkin. Summer, our very lovely dog walker, takes her to the woods once a day, but out on the balcony is Pumpkin's favourite place in the world. When she isn't dozing in the sunshine on the plush furniture, she's tearing around from one end to the other and throwing her mountain of toys in the air. I pause for a moment to watch her exploring the flowerbeds and find myself marvelling at how she really is the perfect addition to our family. The final piece of the Morgan puzzle.

Too busy staring at Pumpkin through the window, I almost don't spot Noah when he reappears in the hallway, still very much in his crazy outfit.

'Noah!' I exclaim, taking an apple from the fridge and slamming the door. 'I thought I told you to change!'

'But Gee-Gee said I could wear this.' He adjusts his mask and pretends to fire web at the ceiling. 'Take that!' He yells, rolling around on the floor like a stunt double.

'Oh, really?' Resting my hand on my hip, I exhale sharply. 'And what exactly did she say?'

Noah giggles and jumps to his feet. 'She said... she said that you're stupid and jeans are boring!'

Pursing my lips to stop myself from screaming, I calmly fasten his lunchbox and march him back into his room. After forcing him out of his costume and into a pair of jeans. I instruct him to wait in the living room and go off in search of Janie. Quickly finding her wrapped up in a duvet with a face mask over her eyes, she doesn't even realise that I've come into her room. Deliberately kicking the door closed with a bang, I yank open the curtains and wait for her to come around.

'What the...' Sitting bolt upright, she tears off her face mask and scowls. 'What the hell is wrong with you? Can't you see I'm sleeping here?'

'Why did you tell Noah he could wear a *pirate costume* to nursery?' I hiss, folding my arms and taking a step towards her.

'He's going to *nursery*, Clara. Not a meeting with the damn Queen.' Tugging her mask back on, she slips beneath the sheets and rolls over. 'Give the boy a break!'

'I don't care *where* he's going!' I fire back, rage bubbling in the pit of my stomach. 'And whilst we're at it, do not call me stupid to my child ever again!'

Janie sticks a hand out from beneath the duvet and flips me the bird. I am about to launch into an angry tirade when my phone starts ringing in the other room. Throwing my arms in the air, I swear under my breath and march back into the kitchen. Now sulking in his *boring* clothes, Noah is refusing to look at me. Digging my handset from the depths of my handbag, I let Pumpkin back into the apartment and usher Noah to the front door.

'Hello?' I grumble into the handset, taking Noah's hand and heading for the stairs.

'Clara?' Eve's familiar voice floats down the line and I brace myself for what I am about to hear. 'It's Eve...'

Eve *never* calls before work. Unless it's to say that she's having an emergency duvet day, which roughly translates to... *I'm tying Owen to the bed in a desperate bid to fall pregnant.* Throwing Noah onto my hip, I take the steps two at a time until I reach the next floor.

'What's up?' I manage, holding the phone between my ear and shoulder.

'I just wanted to tell you to skip breakfast.' The line crackles and I wander over to the window for a better signal. 'I'm at the deli on Smith Street.'

I pause for a moment, not being quite sure if I have heard her correctly. For one Eve lives in this building, so I have absolutely no idea why she's at Smith Street which is way across town and second of all, Eve doesn't exactly eat breakfast. Eve gets up at 5am for a yoga class and then tucks into a bowl of natural yoghurt. Cream cheese bagels and bacon sandwiches aren't exactly on her agenda.

'OK...' I respond slowly, beckoning Noah to knock on Gina's door. 'Thanks.'

Eve mutters something about the best bagels in town and ends the call, just as Gina throws open the door.

'Hey!' She smiles brightly and steps aside for Noah and I to come inside.

Still not happy at being forced to change out of his pirate outfit, Noah scowls at Gina and pushes past her.

'Blimey!' Gina raises her eyebrows and holds out her hand for Noah's lunchbox. 'Someone got out on the wrong side of bed this morning!'

Smiling apologetically, I let out a sigh and scratch the tip of my nose. 'He wanted to come as Spiderman today. Well, Spiderman slash Jack Sparrow...'

Gina widens her already huge green eyes and laughs. 'Been there! Melrose refused to leave the house yesterday without her fairy wings and tiara. I had to sit with the bank manager whilst she threw fairy dust over our accountant.'

I let out a giggle and shake my head. 'Kids! Who'd have them?'

Gina laughs along and winces as a high-pitched scream erupts from the living room.

'What's going on in there?' She hollers over her shoulder. 'Remember, Melrose, you're on your last warning!'

Trying not to laugh, I glance at my watch as Gina's eldest, Madison, appears behind her.

'MJ threw orange juice on my backpack!' Scrunching her pretty face up into a frown, Madison tosses her black curls over her shoulder and stamps her feet furiously.

Sensing that a whole world of chaos is about to erupt, I plan to make my escape when a thought suddenly hits me. 'Before I forget, Eve did fill you in about Friday, didn't she?'

Gina nods animatedly, her hoop earrings jangling as she ushers Madison back into the living room. 'She did and I cannot wait!'

'Me neither. I'll see you later!' With a quick wave, I zip up my coat and head back down the hallway to the stairs.

Taking the steps two at a time, I make it to the ground floor quickly and push my way out into the real world. Joining the lines of marching people, I make a mental note to pick up Oliver's dry cleaning on my lunch hour. A frisson of annoyance runs through me as I picture Janie lounging around whilst I rush around like a headless chicken. She's never been maternal, Oliver is the first person to admit that, but I never imagined she could be so bloody bone idle. In the time that she has been with us, I don't think I've seen her lift a finger once. She hasn't ever offered to help with the dishes, she turns her nose up when I ask her to accompany me to the supermarket and to say that she's untidy would be the world's biggest understatement.

A pang of sadness hits my chest as I picture the state of our spare bedroom. The once immaculate space now resembles something from a disaster movie, with the remnants of the catastrophe strewn around for the world to see. Knickers hang from the beautiful chandelier, empty bottles of Jack litter the ornate dressing table and things that I can't even repeat hide beneath the Egyptian cotton sheets. I've lost count of the number of times that I've attempted to clear away her mess, only for Oliver to scold me for *invading her personal space*. How can I possibly invade her space when she is already invading mine?

Dodging a couple of tourists who are snapping away with their long lens cameras, I dig my lip balm out of my pocket and apply a thick layer to my chapped lips. Our one saving grace with the demise of Janie's marriage is that Oliver's dad, Randy, is now blissfully happy. When they first went their separate ways, Randy struck up a relationship with a bubbly young blonde thing named Courtney. At first, we were all rather cynical, but time keeps ticking by and they are still going strong. After spending their first few months together travelling the Bahamas, Randy and Courtney settled in Austin, Texas and they've been wrapped up in each other ever since. Oh, how I wish Janie would bugger off to the Caribbean for a while. I'd even buy her a ticket. One way, of course.

Coming to a stop outside Floral Fizz, I spot Eve through the glass and raise my hand. Her blue eyes sparkle as her perfect pink pout stretches into a model worthy smile. If I didn't love Eve, I could so easily hate her. Only Eve could pull off gym wear and pink trainers without looking like an extra from a Little Britain sketch. I look down at my black trousers and white shirt and shake my head. No, I'm definitely more Vicky Pollard than Victoria's Secret.

In my rush to get to work on time, I never pause to take in just how stunning Floral Fizz actually is. Unlike most florists', the exterior of the shop is almost as beautiful as the interior. When Owen purchased this place it was pretty much derelict, and Eve spent months designing each and every detail. Not satisfied with making it gorgeous on the inside, Eve went above and beyond ensuring that the entrance was equally as spectacular. Taking inspiration from a classic wedding arch, the doorway to the shop is situated between two ivory pillars, which have been adorned with stunning paintings of lush green ivy, pretty butterflies and bright flowers. I've lost count of the number of people who stop in their tracks to take photos as they hustle along the street. It's fair to say that Floral Fizz has become somewhat of a landmark here on Teller Street.

Snapping out of my musing, I tug my handbag onto my shoulder and release the door handle. The familiar twinkly chime rings loudly as I use my hips to push my way inside. Letting out a squeal, Eve steps out from behind the counter and pulls me towards her with gym-honed arms.

'Have I got a treat for you!' Her eyes glint as she drags me across the shop floor.

'OK...' I mumble cautiously, confused as to what could possibly await me.

Allowing her to lead me into the storeroom, my eyes widen as I take in the scene in front of me. An incredible selection of bagels, pastries, fruit and muffins cover the worktops, creating a rather yummy looking breakfast buffet.

'Ta-da!' She exclaims, jumping up and down on the spot like a giddy child. 'Well, what do you think?'

'I think... I think that's a lot of food...' I manage at last, taking a sideways glance at Eve and wondering what on earth is going on. 'Do we have an open day today that I've forgotten about?' My body momentarily freezes as I rack my brains frantically. 'Is there a wedding party coming in?'

Eve lets out a dainty giggle and shakes her blonde bob. 'No, nothing at all. This is just my way of saying *thank you* for being such a fabulous member of staff and above all, a truly wonderful friend.'

Feeling a little shell shocked, I manage a stunned smile as she pulls me towards her and squeezes tightly. I attempt to remove her hair from my lip balm and get a waft of her eye-wateringly expensive perfume.

'That's so nice of you...' I gush, still not sure as to why she bought so much food. 'Although I think you may have gone a tad overboard on the bagels...'

Eve shakes off my comment with a laugh and pulls out two chairs. 'Well, what are you waiting for? Dig in!'

Shaking my head at her bizarre behaviour, I tug off my jacket and hang it on the back of the seat. The smell of freshly cooked bread makes my mouth salivate as I try to decide what to go for first.

'How did you get on with the baby-making yesterday?' I ask, selecting a poppy seeded bagel and smothering it in cream cheese.

A flash of sadness hits her eyes before she covers it with a smile. 'Well, we gave it three goes and then I spent the rest of the day in a very uncomfortable Yoga pose...'

My mind flits to my Yoga manual as I try to picture exactly which Yoga pose she is referring to. If I was to take a guess, I would imagine it is something that involves contorting her uterus a hundred and eighty degrees. Taking a sip of my coffee, I offer her a sympathetic smile and reach for a napkin.

'How long has it been now?' I ask cautiously, not wanting her to get upset like she did last time.

'Twenty-two months.' Eve adjusts her sports leggings and sticks out her bottom lip. 'We must have had sex *hundreds* of times. I just don't get it. You have sex and you make a baby. Why isn't it happening?'

I lean over and place a reassuring hand on her incredibly toned thigh. 'Don't beat yourself up about it. It will happen for you, I know it.'

'But when?' She laughs hysterically and twists her giant bridal set around her finger. 'It's just so unfair. Look at you and Oliver. You weren't even *trying* to get pregnant.' I open my mouth to speak, but Eve carries on talking regardless. 'And Gina, she keeps popping them out like peanuts. I mean, what's *wrong* with me?'

'*Nothing* is wrong with you!' I exclaim, dropping my bagel into a napkin and sliding over to her. 'Look at you. If anyone was built to make a baby, it's you.'

The fact that someone like Eve is struggling to conceive really is a total mystery to me. Her fitness routine is enough to make most personal trainers squirm and not a crumb passes her lips that doesn't provide one health benefit or another. She really is the perfect example of someone who treats their body like a temple. From sunrise jogging sessions in the park to colonic irrigations and enough vitamins to feed a football team, Eve puts more care and attention into her fitness than most people put into their children.

To add salt to the wound, ever since she put her mind to having a baby, Eve upped the ante on her already extreme regime. Gone are her famous dinner parties, gone are the seven-course taster meals and her once platinum locks are now a good few shades darker than they were a couple of years back. As only Eve could, she didn't feel comfortable with polluting her body with hair bleaching chemicals when she was trying to form a new life. On her mission to conceive she has followed all the rules, read every book and hasn't strayed from the guidelines once. It's actually incredibly sad.

'I feel like I'm being punished...' She whispers, dropping her head and letting out a little sob.

'Punished?' My brow furrows into a frown as she erupts into a series of mouse-like cries. 'What on earth could you be *punished* for?'

Eve brings her eyes up to meet mine and I spot a tear rolling down her cheek. 'For you know... my past.'

I exhale slowly and shake my head in response. If you aren't already aware, Eve's life hasn't always been quite as glamorous as it is today. Born in a rather unfortunate part of town, Eve had to beg, borrow and steal her way through her teenage years in order to survive. One wrong turn led to another and before she knew what she was doing, Eve got involved with a rather bad crowd. As a means of funding the lifestyle that she wanted, Eve turned to the rather seedy world of escorting. I know, it sounds terrible, but she wasn't a prostitute, I would like to make that quite clear. All she did was accompany rich men to corporation dinners and prestige events. Hardly the biggest crime in the world. In fact, it's not a crime at all from a legal perspective, but not everyone was as quick to forgive Eve for providing such services. Needless to say, Eve wishes she could erase this portion of her past and has never been able to fully forgive herself for it.

'Don't be silly!' I exclaim, grabbing a napkin and dabbing at her damp eyes. 'We've all done things we wish we could take back and some a lot worse than what you did...'

Eve grabs a tissue and nods slowly. There's absolutely nothing worse than seeing your friends beat themselves up. I'm about to tell her to stop kicking herself about things she can't change when the antique clock on the wall chimes loudly. Immediately jumping to her feet, Eve shakes away her tears and grabs an apron off the rack.

'I'll go and open up.' She pulls a tiny compact mirror out of her pocket and quickly tops up her makeup. 'You stay back here. Enjoy the breakfast and I'll give you a shout if we get busy.'

Flashing me a smile that doesn't quite reach her eyes, Eve slips into the shop, leaving me feeling rather emotional. Poor Eve. Life can be *so* unfair sometimes. I take a sip of coffee and my mind drifts back to Janie. Way to go, Clara. Here I am grumbling about my slothful mother-in-law when my dear friend is breaking her heart about possibly being infertile. Suddenly feeling a little guilty, I put down my paper cup and start clearing away the food. As I wrap the remaining muffins in tinfoil, I get to thinking about just how good a friend Eve has been to me over the past few years. Apart from a slight misunderstanding at the start of our relationship, Eve and I have never had a cross word. If my time on this planet has taught me anything, it's that good friends are hard to find, harder to leave and impossible to forget.

Hearing voices on the shop floor, I poke my head around the door and watch Eve serve an elderly woman. Ever the professional, all evidence of her meltdown has disappeared and in place of her tears is a bright smile. To look at her now you would never believe that just five minutes ago she was crying into a kale and mint smoothie. I don't think I've ever met anybody as strong as Eve in my entire life. Throughout all the heartache and tears that have brought her to where she is today, Eve has never complained once. Never has she used her past to her advantage and in all the years I've known her she hasn't ever felt sorry for herself.

Deciding to make it my mission to put a spring back in her step, I grab my apron and tie it around my waist. After a final sip of my coffee, I take a deep breath and march out onto the shop floor. Flicking on the radio, I scour through the channels for something upbeat. Feel good music fills the room and inevitably catches Eve's attention. Tapping my fingers on the counter, I pretend that I haven't noticed and replace the till roll.

'I *love* this song!' She squeals excitedly as she waves goodbye to her first customer of the day.

'Really?' I shrug my shoulders nonchalantly and spin around to face her. 'I had no idea...'

Hitting me on the arm, she hums the lyrics happily. 'You *know* this is one of my favourites!'

Bopping around on the spot, Eve grabs a single rose and holds it between her teeth. I can't help but laugh as she sashays back and forth, attempting to sing along with her lips clamped around the flower stem. Turning on her heels, she runs towards me and begins to spin me around the shop floor. I let out a giggle which quickly develops into a full-on belly laugh. The throngs of people buzzing along the street outside stop and stare at the crazy women who are dancing around to cheesy classics before 9am. Not giving them a second glance, I throw back my head and shout out the lyrics like we are completely alone.

Eve closes her eyes, losing herself in the music and for those few minutes... she is free.

Chapter 4

'Eve was *really* upset today.' Taking a big slug of Rioja, I lean back on the couch and swirl the red liquid around my glass. 'I felt so bad for her.'

My head sinks into the soft cushions and I exhale loudly. What started as a gentle waltz around the florist's soon escalated into a fiery tango involving three wedding parties and a disgruntled widow. Seriously, working in that florist's is like munching through a bag of Revels, you just don't know what you're going to get next.

'I dunno what to say.' Oliver scratches the back of his neck and lets out a sigh. 'Owen was pretty beat up at golf last week, too.'

I shrug in response and look down at Pumpkin, who is happily taking the eyes out of her latest chew toy. Catching me looking at her, she immediately jumps to her feet and gives me her best *please let me on the couch* eyes. Shaking my head, I last a full thirty seconds before relenting and pulling her onto my lap. Immediately getting herself comfortable, she rests her wet snout on my stomach and closes her eyes happily.

'It must be putting such a strain on their marriage.' I muse, draining the contents of my glass and placing it on the coffee table.

'I'm sure it is.' Oliver leans over and scratches Pumpkin's soft belly. 'They have been trying for years now.'

'I wish there were something we could do to help them...' I let out a yawn and close my eyes, breathing deeply from my stomach.

'Unfortunately, this is one of those situations in life where we are powerless to help.' Oliver drags my legs onto his knees and starts to massage my feet.

Rushing around the florist's all day has meant that my previously soft and manicured tootsies are now in desperate need of a pedicure. Peeling open my eyes, I look down at my chipped red polish and kick myself for missing my appointment at the spa. There's no way that I could step out in flip flops like this. I'd rather melt in my Converse than reveal these trotters to the world.

Just as I am dozing off, Oliver hits a ticklish spot on my heel and I let out a squeal.

'Sorry!' He laughs and holds up his hands in apology. 'That was an accident, I swear!'

I grin at my lovely husband and wiggle my toes. 'Shouldn't this be the other way around?' I ask, recalling our earlier conversation about just how busy things have been for him at work lately.

He sighs and I rub his leg encouragingly. If you don't already know, Oliver works at Suave, a luxury label supplying shoes and handbags to the fashion industry. What started as a temporary contract many years ago soon transpired into promotion after promotion and Oliver has been a permanent fixture ever since. Suave has actually played a huge part in our lives as it's not only where Oliver and I met, it's also where I met Lianna, Marc, Gina and many more of our friends. Over the years most of us broke away from the Suave family, but Oliver has been with the firm since the day we met. After a quick detour to

Australia, Marc reprised his role as manager and has taken the company from strength to strength. I still find myself reminiscing about the good old days when we all worked together. Think Sex and the City crossed with The Office and you have half an idea of just how much fun we all had.

'Don't you miss the days when we all worked together?' A smile plays on my lips as my mind drifts to our past antics. 'Can you believe how much has changed for everyone since back then? It's like we're not even the same people anymore.'

Oliver glances up at the family portrait on the wall and gives my foot a squeeze. 'Things sure are a lot different now, huh? I guess we have a lot to thank Suave for.'

Looking down at Pumpkin, I get to thinking about what my life would be like if I had never applied for that job. The job that led to me having my best friends, my husband and my beautiful baby boy. It's like all the wrong turns I took previous to this were meant to lead me to where I am today.

'We certainly do...' I whisper, burying my head in the cushions.

Allowing my eyes to close, I am seconds away from falling into a much-needed sleep when the front door slams shut. Visibly jumping in my seat, I peel open my eyes to see Janie steadying herself on the kitchen island. With mascara smeared down her cheeks, the remnants of what appears to be a kebab on her dress and the undeniable stench of whiskey drifting off her, she is clearly paralytic. Locking eyes with Oliver, I choose to say nothing and bite my lip as anger bubbles in my chest.

Clearly not picking up on my repulsion, Oliver grins widely at her and laughs. 'Well, it looks like you had a good night?' He pushes my legs off his lap and motions for his intoxicated mother to join us.

'It was *fantastic...*' She slurs, waving her arms around like she is still in whatever dingy bar she's just crawled out of.

Reaching into the cabinet for the Jack Daniel's, she clumsily grabs three glasses and stumbles into the living room, dropping splashes of bourbon onto the floor as she goes. The floor that I spent forty minutes scrubbing when I came home from an eight-hour shift. Taking deep breaths so that I don't spontaneously combust with fury, I chew the inside of my cheek as she comes very close to smashing my best crystal.

'We went to Lightning.' Janie sniggers as though she is telling a joke and fills the glasses with a shaky hand.

Lightning? I feel my face pull into a scowl as I try to picture my mother-in-law in a hip-hop nightclub. Seriously, who does she think she is? Miley bloody Cyrus?

'We?' Oliver questions, taking a glass from the table and clinking it against Janie's.

'Rose.' Janie mumbles, grabbing her glass with both hands and pushing the third towards to me.

'My *mum?*' I exclaim, unable to contain my horror. 'You took my *mum* to a nightclub frequented with wannabe gangsters and gold-diggers?'

Oliver lets out a loud laugh and I fight the overwhelming urge to hit him with my shoe.

'Oh, lighten up, Clara!' He throws an arm around my tense shoulders and tickles my chin. 'It's just a bit of fun...'

'*Lighten!*' Janie squeals, banging her hand down on the table. 'Do you get it? *Lighten*, as in, *Lightning!*'

Oliver joins in with her hysterics and I usher Pumpkin to the floor. Rolling off the couch, I grab my phone and shove my feet into Oliver's slippers.

'I'm going to check on Noah.' I let out a fake yawn and squeeze past Janie's bandy legs in a strop.

'Come on! Don't leave!' Oliver makes a grab for my arm, but I snatch it out of his reach. 'Have a drink with us!'

Ignoring their protests, I slip into our bedroom and close the door quietly behind me. I don't need to check on Noah as I can see him snoozing on the baby monitor, I just wanted an excuse to get away from Janie. She's a handful when sober, but drunk she verges on completely *impossible*. I genuinely can't be around her when she is in that state. Collapsing into a heap on the bed, I tug the duvet over my head in a poor bid to block out the image of my mum and Janie twerking whilst throwing back shooters. What the hell is my mum playing at? She's leaving for a cruise tomorrow morning!

Listening to the two of them laugh as Janie reveals all about her *fabulous* evening, I find myself recalling all the times Oliver has blown his top at his mother's disgraceful tricks. What on earth has changed for him in the past six months to make him find her impudent behaviour acceptable? Is he going through a midlife crisis and reliving his youth through her? Has he had a secret lobotomy that I don't know about? I just don't get it!

As I am mentally cursing Janie into oblivion, a tiny scratching at the door catches my attention. I try to ignore it, but the pawing is soon accompanied by a familiar cry. Begrudgingly getting up, I allow myself a delicious stretch before padding across the room and releasing the handle. A wet nose pokes its way inside, quickly followed by a golden coat and a shiny tail that is wagging rapidly.

'Do you want to escape the chaos too, Pumpkin?' Closing the door, I switch off the main light and flick on the lamp.

Grabbing her toy, she curls up on the floor and rolls onto her back, wriggling around like the happy puppy she is. The noise from the living room turns up a notch and I silently count to ten. Rubbing my tired eyes, I wander into our bathroom and perch on the rim of the bath. When Janie takes me to the edge of insanity, this is my happy place. The place where I can escape reality, even if it is just for half an hour. I scan the rack of toiletries and my hands land on my favourite jasmine bath oil. Flipping open the lid, I turn on both taps and proceed to pour the shimmering liquid into the running water.

Silently mesmerised by the sound of the water as it thrashes down into the tub, I almost don't hear my phone ringing in the bedroom. Grabbing a towel to dry my hands, I make it to the bed just in time to see Lianna's name flashing up on the display. Jabbing at the handset, I flop down onto the bed and grab my glasses from the dresser. A few moments later, her face pops up on the screen and I instantly feel a pang of longing.

'Hey!' She smiles brightly and I can't help but notice that she is holding her iPhone just inches from her face. 'How's it going?'

'Not bad.' I nod as I speak, my foot automatically tapping in time to the reggae music in the background. 'How are you?'

'I'm great! *Really* great!' She takes off her aviator sunglasses and I can tell from the mischievous look playing on her lips that she's hiding something. 'Listen, I've got something to tell you...'

I knew it! Squinting my eyes at the screen suspiciously, I slip off the bed and walk back into the bathroom. 'Is it good or bad?'

'Good...' She props up her handset on the table in front of her and I let out a scream.

'Lianna!' I yell, almost toppling into the bathtub with shock. 'Your hair!'

'Oh, that...' She twirls around to let me see the extent of her extreme new haircut.

My jaw drops open as I take in my best friend's new look. For as long as I have known her, Li has always had long blonde locks. The kind of blonde that made you stop in your tracks. Shades of caramel, honey and butterscotch would melt together as she walked, causing her to be the envy of women everywhere. Now she's rocking a choppy bob, but what is the most shocking is that her blonde tresses are now a stunning shade of pink. It's edgy, it's unique, it's... *fabulous!*

'Do you like it?' She asks, between sips of her brightly coloured cocktail.

'I *love* it...' I gasp, trying to get used to her new style. 'It's just so different! What made you do it?'

'Julianne came into The Hangout last week and I fell in love with her hair, so you know, I thought I would steal her style.' She raises her eyebrows and stretches out in her seat.

'Julianne?' I repeat, turning off the taps and perching on the toilet seat. 'The dancer?' Lianna nods in response and I suddenly see the resemblance. 'Oh yeah! I totally see it now. Well, it looks fantastic. I love it.'

Placing the screen face down whilst I strip off and climb into the tub, I rearrange the bubbles before balancing the handset behind the taps.

'So, I was going to tell you something...' Her eyes sparkle as her face breaks into a smile. 'You know how it's our anniversary in a couple of weeks?' I nod in response and tip my head back to allow the ends of my hair to soak through. 'Well, Vernon and I are going to take a vacation to celebrate.'

'A vacation to where?' I splutter, wiping my eyes and reaching for the shower gel. 'You already live in paradise.'

Disappearing from view, Li reappears with an envelope and holds a plane ticket up to the screen. Leaning forward for a closer look, my jaw drops open as I take in the text.

'Heathrow?' I squeal, splashing around in the water. 'You're coming to London?'

'I am!' She screams happily and waves her tickets around in the air. 'Vernon surprised me with the news last night!'

'This is amazing!' Clasping my hands to my face, I try to stop my heart from racing. 'When?'

'Umm...' She glances down at the tickets and squints. 'Two weeks tomorrow!'

We shriek simultaneously and inadvertently catch Pumpkin's attention. Obviously wanting to get involved in the jovialities, she creeps up to the bath and puts two paws on the side of the tub.

'Did you hear that, Pumpkin?' Turning the screen to her face, I let out a giggle as she licks the phone. 'Auntie Lianna is coming to see you!'

'I certainly am!' Li cries, clapping her hands together. 'You have *no* idea how excited I am.'

'Believe me, I know *exactly* how excited you are because I am equally as excited!' Making a grab for my shampoo, I squirt a dollop onto my head and start to lather up. 'Seriously, Li, I have missed you so much. It's been *so* long...'

'I know...' A wave of guilt washes over her face and she smiles sadly. 'I've missed you, too. But you know, it's a lot easier to deal with when you wake up to this every day...'

Flipping the camera around, she wanders over to the window and shows me the incredible view from her bedroom. I let out a whimper as the beautiful Barbados sunshine beams down onto the stunning blue ocean, teasing you in with a twinkle. A pang of envy runs through me and I stick out my tongue.

'Don't rub it in.' I grumble, fumbling around on the windowsill for my face mask.

Lianna laughs and turns the screen back to her. 'Vernon's like a giddy child. He's never been to England before. He wants to hit up *all* the tourist spots.'

I apply a layer of detoxifying clay to my t-zone as I picture Vernon dragging Lianna on an open-top bus tour. 'Just make sure he brings some suitable clothing. From next week, summer will be officially *over*.'

'The good old British weather is certainly going to be a shock to him!' Li laughs and drains the contents of her cocktail. 'It's been so hot here lately, he won't know what's hit him.'

'Neither will you! You've been gone for so long...'

She nods in agreement and looks out to sea. 'I love it here, really love it, but lately, I must admit that I've been missing home just a little.'

A selfish part of me loves hearing Lianna refer to London as *home*. I know that she's lived in Barbados for years now, but telling myself that she is just on an extended holiday makes it easier for me to deal with.

'You know, you coming over here is going to cheer Eve up so much.' Rubbing exfoliator into my cheeks, I readjust the bubbles to protect my modesty. 'She has been pretty down lately.'

Lianna sticks out her bottom lip and fiddles with the settings for a better reception. 'No luck with the baby-making yet?'

I shake my head regrettably and slip my shoulders back under the water. 'Afraid not. She's tried every trick in the book, but still nothing.'

'That's so sad.' Li frowns and looks down to the floor. 'Hey, do you know if she's tried healing crystals? Vernon's mum is obsessed with crystal healing and she believes that jade helps to increase fertility.'

'Really?' I scrunch up my nose dubiously and comb conditioner through my hair.

Lianna nods and crashes down onto her bed. 'She swears by it! Honestly, every time I see her she insists on rubbing it on my stomach...' I raise my eyebrows and wonder if she has something to tell me. 'Before you ask, the answer is *no!*' She rolls her eyes and takes another sip of her cocktail. 'I'm quite happy being the world's best auntie, thank you very much. I have absolutely no desire to fill my life with nappies, baby vomit and sleepless nights.'

'You don't have to make it sound so terrible!' I tease, reaching over and stroking Pumpkin's head.

I hate to admit it, but she does have a point. Lianna gets all the cuddles and laughter without any of the poop or tantrums.

'I almost forgot to ask, how are things with Janie?' Li rolls onto her side and yawns. 'Any signs of her moving on yet?'

My mood swiftly changes at the mention of Janie and I am suddenly reminded that she's smashed in my living room, knocking back whiskey with my husband.

'Unfortunately, she's still very much with us...' I hope the manner of my voice is enough for her not to ask any more questions.

'OK...' Lianna mumbles, clearing sensing the tone.

Knowing very well that I could easily ramble on about Janie all night long once I get started, I decide to wrap up the call.

'Well, I should probably let you go. If I don't dry this hair soon, I'm going to look like Medusa.' Shaking my head to emphasise my point, I wince as I splash bubbles into my eye.

Saying our goodbyes, I make sure to reiterate just how happy I am that she is finally tearing herself away from her beloved island to pay us a visit. After the screen bounces back to black, I use my toes to pull the plug and wrap myself up in my waffle robe. Wet droplets land on Pumpkin's nose as she follows me back into the bedroom. Pressing my ear to the door, I can still hear Janie's drunken ramblings, so I decide to call it a night. Quickly exchanging my robe for a nightie, I roughly towel dry my hair before attacking it with my precious diffuser.

With a final check on the baby monitor, I apply a layer of moisturiser to my face and crawl beneath the sheets. Pumpkin waits patiently to be invited onto the bed and I tap the space beside me. Not missing a beat, she fires up and flops down at my feet. Snuggling into my pillow, I recall the day we first brought Pumpkin home. Oliver was adamant that she would never sleep on our bed. He was very much of the mindset that dogs are animals and should be treated as such. It turns out that his harsh words lasted for all of two hours and on her first night with us, she used her big brown eyes to break Oliver down and has been a permanent fixture at the foot of our bed ever since.

Running my fingers through her soft coat, I finally allow myself to relax. Janie might be driving me crazy, but let's look on the bright side, Lianna's coming home! A smile plays on the corner of my lips and I wiggle my toes against the soft bedding. My best friend, who I have spent the last two years missing terribly is finally coming back to see me! We have been over to Barbados numerous times to visit her, but this will be the first time since she left that she will be back on home soil.

A frisson of excitement runs through my veins as I picture the two of us at our old haunts. I hope Vernon is prepared to wave goodbye to his wife for a little while, because for the time that she's here I'm not going to let her out of my sight. Barbados might be where Li lives, but London will always be her home. They say that home is where the heart is, and my heart has felt a little bit empty since the day she left.

Pumpkin creeps towards me and snuggles her face into my belly. Allowing my eyes to close, I find myself counting my blessings. I may have one very audacious mother-in-law who isn't aware when she's outstayed her welcome, but Lianna's coming home and that makes me happy, even if it is just for a little while...

Chapter 5

'Personally, I would go with the spray roses. I think they would set the lilies off beautifully.' Holding open the wedding brochure, I wait for the pickiest customer in the world to make a decision.

'I dunno...' Screwing up her nose, she shakes her red hair and flips through the pages. 'I just don't know if roses say *wedding*. Do you know what I mean?'

Nope. I absolutely do *not* know what she means. Roses have been hailed the classic wedding flower since, well, since forever. I smile through gritted teeth and take back the catalogue. She has dismissed every other flower in the book. Spray roses were my last hope. Where the hell do we go from here?

'How are we getting on?' Dawn appears at my side and flashes Miss Fussy a friendly smile. 'Have you come to a decision?'

'We're getting there...' I give Dawn a look that says we are most certainly *not* getting there and hand her the book. 'Although, perhaps we could do with a second opinion.'

'Sure.' Taking a seat next to me, Dawn looks between the customer and I confidently. 'What have we got so far?'

'Calla lilies.' We answer in unison.

'Great choice!' Dawn gushes enthusiastically. 'One of our most popular wedding flowers.'

I nod in agreement and hope that Dawn has better luck than I've had for the past two hours. Scanning the brochure, Dawn appears deep in thought for a few moments before breaking into a grin.

'OK, how about hydrangeas? We have the most *stunning* lilac hydrangeas...'

'I *hate* hydrangeas.' The customer purses her lips and frowns, clearly disgusted at the idea of having such *hideous* flowers in her bridal bouquet.

'Oh...' Dawn nudges me under the table and I bite my lip to stop myself from laughing. 'Well, I also have some very pretty lilac tulips...'

'I also hate *lilac*.' The fastidious redhead spits out lilac with such venom that I actually wince.

Dawn looks at me perplexed and holds up her bridal breakdown. 'But the notes say that your colour scheme is purple.'

'Exactly!' She snaps, grabbing her handbag and pushing out her seat. 'Purple, not *lilac*.' I exchange panicked glances with Dawn as she shakes on her coat and makes for the door. 'Forget it. This has been a complete waste of my time. I shall use another florist. One that actually knows the difference between *purple* and *lilac*.'

Watching her march down the street, I stare at the spot where she once stood with my jaw wide open.

'Talk about a bridezilla...' Dawn whispers, slamming the wedding catalogue shut and exhaling loudly. 'She was a bloody nightmare!'

'Who was a nightmare?' Eve steps out of the storeroom with a bucket of sunflowers and plonks them onto the counter.

'Clara's customer.' Dawn stretches her tanned arms out above her head and yawns. 'There was just no pleasing her.'

'To be honest, I don't think she knew herself what she wanted.' I spin around to face Eve and drop the bridal breakdown into the bin.

Eve pulls some sweets out of her apron pocket and pops one into her mouth, chewing thoughtfully before throwing a couple over to Dawn and myself. 'Did you try tulips?' She asks, tapping her glossy nails on the counter.

'Yes.' We reply simultaneously.

'Roses?'

'Yes.'

'Hydrangeas?'

'*Yes!*'

'I'm going to save you some time, Eve. We tried *everything!*' Pushing myself to my feet, I check my watch and wander over to the window.

'Oh…' Eve shrugs her shoulders and sighs. 'Well, I hope she finds what she is looking for.'

'I don't…' Dawn grumbles, running her fingers through her mahogany hair.

Eve and I exchange shocked glances and Dawn is quick to defend herself.

'What? She was horrible!'

Not being able to disagree with her, I resort to a stifled giggle as Eve shakes her head disapprovingly. Realising that it's nearing closing time, I lean against the glass and stare outside at the busy street. The resident eccentric lady is perched on her bench, shouting something about the economy to anyone who will listen. Excitement runs through me as I remember that unlike the other six nights of the week, tonight I am not heading home. For this one night, I am not the dishwasher, the laundry-doer, the maid or the toilet cleaner. Tonight, I get to do something a little more enjoyable. Spinning around I flash Eve and Dawn a smile and point to the clock on the wall.

'Fifteen minutes, girls! Have you got that Friday feeling yet?'

* * *

'Thank God it's Friday!' Gina holds out her glass and the rest of us clink our flutes against it.

'Thank God it's Friday!' We echo happily, before taking a sip of the crisp bubbles.

Swooning at the taste, I take a deep breath and exhale slowly. I have waited all week for this one evening and now that it's here, I'm going to savour each and every second.

'Well, we made it through another week!' Dawn giggles and reaches over for the bowl of olives.

'We certainly did. Here's to tonight's book club. I hope it proves as *educational* as all the others!' I wink cheekily as a laugh echoes around the room.

This has to be the best idea that Eve has ever had. Our famous book club is held every Friday evening and has become my favourite part of the week. Kicking back in my seat, I scan my surroundings and feel every muscle in my body start to relax. When Eve and I stumbled across Artemis on our way home one afternoon, we immediately fell in love with its cosy surroundings and quaint interior. The ivory walls are adorned with stunning images of Greek gods and goddesses, making you feel like you've stepped into an extraordinary art gallery. Tipping back my head to take in the intricate drawings, I run my fingers along the stem of my glass and get comfortable in my plush seat.

When Eve suggested that we start a book club, it's fair to say that I wasn't exactly forthcoming with my offer to join. It was only when she revealed that she didn't intend to do any actual *reading* in this club that she pricked my attention. You see, being excused from your daily duties is a lot easier when you have the justification of an educational book club. Telling your husband that you're abandoning him for one evening a week to drink cocktails and dance with your girlfriends generally goes down like a lead balloon, as the four of us soon discovered.

Until Floral Fizz came along, Eve was used to being the very bored housewife of a very rich man. I don't think she quite realised what actual work entailed. After just a couple of months at the florist's, Eve declared that she needed at least one day a week where she could let her hair down and have some *me* time. With Floral Fizz being my first job since I had Noah, I must admit that I was also finding it a little demanding and the thought of a club for women who felt the same seemed right up my street. As it turns out, our club ended up consisting of just four members. Eve, Dawn, Gina and myself, but I wouldn't want it any other way.

'So, does anyone have any gossip to share?' Gina asks, adjusting her tiny sequin dress and throwing back her bubbles.

Not wanting to give up my juicy piece of Lianna information just yet, I purse my lips and wait to see if anyone else speaks up first. Realising that no one has anything to offer, I decide to reveal all.

'Actually, I have some pretty exciting news...' Placing my glass on the table, I take in the three pairs of wide eyes that are staring at me in anticipation.

'I know what it is!' Dawn suddenly exclaims, jumping to her feet. 'You're pregnant!'

'No!' I yell loudly, a little offended that Dawn thinks I look like I'm with child. 'If I were pregnant do you really think I would be knocking back Champagne?'

'Oh, yeah...' Dawn smiles apologetically and sits back down, looking slightly embarrassed.

Shaking my head at her, I glance over at Eve who looks down at the ground sadly. Bloody hell. I keep forgetting that anything baby related is off limits when Eve is around. She would kill me for saying that, but I can't stand the hurt look that washes across her face. She doesn't even know that she's doing it which makes it a million times worse.

'What is it then?' Gina asks, tapping her feet in time to the music and bringing me back to the subject in question.

'Well...' I drum my fingers on the table to build up the momentum and hold my breath. 'Lianna's coming home!'

'Oh my God!' Eve squeals, putting down her orange juice. 'When?'

I let out a laugh and shift around in my seat. 'It's just for a short visit, but she lands in a couple of weeks.'

An excited buzz echoes around the room and I sit back and revel in their enthusiasm. Watching my friends chatter animatedly amongst themselves, I can't help but feel a little like Santa Claus. It's like Christmas has come early. I knew this would lift everyone's spirits! I almost forget that Lianna isn't just *my* friend and that the others miss her just as much as I do.

'This is fantastic!' Gina motions to the barman that we will have another round of fizz and fluffs up her black hair. 'I've missed that girl so bloody much.'

'We all have!' Eve sighs and perches on the arm of my chair. 'I haven't seen her for almost a year now.'

'Me neither.' I add, recalling the last time that I went to Barbados.

'Count yourselves lucky.' Gina scoffs and slips the barman a wad of notes. 'Marc and I haven't seen her since she left!'

We sit in a strange silence for a moment as we cast our thoughts to our dear friend.

'I am so glad that Li met Vernon.' Gina muses, swapping her empty glass for a full one. 'She's had some awful boyfriends in the past...'

'Really?' Eve turns to face Gina and waits for her to elaborate further.

As Gina fills Eve in on Lianna's dating disasters, I slide over to Dawn and place the olives between us.

'You're going to love Li.' I give her a friendly smile and pop an olive into my mouth.

'To be honest, I feel like I know her already! You guys talk about her all the time!' She giggles and turns a deep shade of pink as a gorgeous man in a navy suit walks by and blatantly checks her out.

'Was he checking me out?' She gasps, straining her neck for a better look at the mystery man.

'I think he was!' A rush of adrenaline runs through me as she reaches out and squeezes my arm.

Frantically looking around in her purse, she pulls out a compact mirror and tops up her lipstick. 'How's my hair?'

I give her a quick once over and nod in response. 'It's perfect! You look amazing.'

She really does. Wearing a nude, lace dress with her glossy hair cascading down her back in a series of perfect curls, she looks almost unrecognisable from the woman who trims the roses at work. I don't think most of our customers would know her from Adam if they saw her right now. That's one of my favourite things about this book club, it gives us a chance to see one another without the obligatory apron or mum jeans. When you see someone every day in a working environment, you almost forget that they're a real person out of office hours.

'How's that delightful mother-in-law of yours doing?' Dawn shouts over the music, which is now noticeably higher than it was ten minutes ago. 'I'm actually surprised that she isn't here tonight.'

'Don't get me started on Janie.' I growl, already knowing that I have sunk enough to go on a drunken rampage. 'She is literally driving me up the wall. I don't know how much more I can take...' Dawn nods knowingly and opens her mouth to speak, but I carry on regardless. 'She came home drunk last night, *again*. That's the third time this week.'

'Wow...' Dawn's eyes widen as my voice gets higher.

'Did I tell you that she brought a guy home on Tuesday?' She shakes her head and covers her mouth in shock. 'And on the way home the other night, she was chatting up the delivery guy from the pizza place on Alton Lane.'

'Pizza Navona?' Eve chips in and I am suddenly aware that she and Gina are listening in on our conversation.

'Yes!' I raise my glass and narrowly avoid spilling it over Dawn's dress.

'You don't mean Francesco, do you?' Eve whispers in horror, looking over her shoulder as though she is half expecting him to be standing behind her.

I nod and take a sip of my fizz as Eve recoils, obviously as disgusted as I am.

'Am I the only one who thinks Francesco is a little cute?' Gina digs out her phone and blinks at the screen, oblivious to the fact that the rest of us are staring at her in shock.

'What?' She yells, hiding her grin behind her glass. 'He is.'

'Anyway…' Dawn glares at Gina and shakes her head. 'Cute or not, I am sure we can all agree that Janie is well out of order.'

'Definitely.' Eve tucks her blonde bob behind her ears and adjusts the hem of her skirt. 'I remember when we had Owen's mother living with us. I swear, it nearly pushed us to breaking point.'

'Really?' I lean forward in a bid to block out the music. 'Was she as bad as Janie?'

Eve purses her lips and taps her wedding band on the rim of her glass. 'I'll admit she wasn't as *obvious* as Janie, but she was absolutely awful.'

'What did she do?' Dawn asks, finishing the last of the olives.

'What *didn't* she do more like! She would belittle me in front of Owen, tell everyone who would listen that I was a gold-digger and not a day went by that she didn't make sure I knew *exactly* what she thought of me.'

'That's awful!' I visibly wince and look at Gina and Dawn for their reactions. 'I can't believe Owen would let her treat you like that.'

Eve shrugs her shoulders and takes a sip of her orange juice. 'Owen was completely ignorant to her behaviour.'

A pang of understanding resonates with me as my mind flits to my own husband. 'That's exactly the same with Oliver.'

'See, that's what I find weird.' Gina sighs and picks up the cocktail menu. 'For all the years I've known Oliver, he's hated Janie's outlandish behaviour more than anyone.'

'Exactly!' I slur, suddenly aware that I might have had one too many. 'For some inexplicable reason, they've become the best of friends! That's what makes it so infuriating. I feel like the bitch wife who's stuck in the middle of their new-found friendship.'

'I think we've all been there!' Gina laughs loudly and beckons over the barman.

'Not me!' Dawn waves her hands around to show off her bare ring finger.

'So, you *are* single?' The handsome man from earlier props himself up at the bar behind us and passes the barman a card.

The three of us glare at Dawn enviously as she seems to lose the ability to speak. Giving her a quick dig in the ribs, Gina stands to her feet and physically drags Dawn over to the bar.

'This is Dawn.' Gina rests her heavily tanned hand on her hip and smacks her lips together. 'She's thirty-six...'

'Thirty-four.' Dawn corrects, suddenly regaining the use of her tongue.

'She's *thirty-four*.' Gina repeats suspiciously, shooting the gorgeous stranger a wink. 'She's single and she's looking for a good time...'

'Gina!' Dawn hisses, playfully hitting her on the arm.

Letting out a laugh, Dawn's admirer holds out his hand. 'I'm Hugh, it's a pleasure to meet you, Dawn.'

His voice is low and husky as he takes her hand in his and smiles broadly. I don't even need to look back at Eve to know that she is swooning, too. Motioning for Gina to leave them alone, I order a few cocktails with the barman and deliberately move further along the bar. As he whips up our drinks, I can't help but peek at Dawn out of the corner of my eye. After a pretty uneventful love life, Dawn had a whirlwind relationship with a man from Brighton. She was so blissfully happy until it turned out that her new-found love already had a lifelong love of his own. After six months of romantic dinners and trips to the seaside, Samuel revealed that he was actually married. Although she didn't let it show, Dawn was devastated and swore herself off men for good, so it's fabulous to see her getting back in the saddle.

The barman places our glasses down in front of us, but I don't think I can face it. My head is starting to hurt from all the fizz and even though I don't have work tomorrow, I'm very aware that I have a little boy who's going to be expecting a visit to the park at 9am. Clearly not having the same worries, Gina plonks herself down on a stool and picks up her glass.

'Do you want mine?' I ask, pushing it towards her. 'I think I've had enough.'

'Don't be soft!' Gina scoffs. 'Besides, one more won't hurt you. You're already wasted!' She throws back her head and cackles, almost toppling off her seat in the process.

Eve sips her drink smugly and I can't help but feel a little envious. Her abstinence from alcohol might mean that she doesn't kick back with the rest of us on a Friday, but it *does* mean she'll wake up as fresh as a daisy tomorrow whilst we are nursing hangovers.

'I say we go on to Lightning!' Gina hoots, waving her arms around in the air to the music. 'What do you say?'

'Hell no!' My stomach churns as I remember where my mum was last night. 'I'm going home after this and you are, too.'

'It looks like you're not the only one...' Eve points over my shoulder at Dawn and I spin around to see her getting her coat from the cloakroom.

'Is she leaving with him?' My jaw drops open as Dawn makes her way over to us. 'Are you *leaving* with him?' I gasp, biting my finger to stop myself from squealing out loud.

'Hugh's invited me to Satin for a nightcap.' Her eyes sparkle as she turns and waves at him. 'Do you guys mind if I...'

'No!' The three of us yell at once, steering her towards the exit.

'Go! Have fun and call me in the morning!' Giving her a squeeze, I wipe a smudge of mascara from beneath her left eye.

'Have a fabulous time, Dawn. You deserve it!' Eve kisses her on both cheeks and shoots her the thumbs-up sign.

Taking a deep breath, she turns on her heels and flashes Gina a glare as she lets out a wolf whistle.

'Don't do anything I wouldn't do!' Gina shouts, laughing so hard that her boobs bounce around in her dress. 'And whatever you do, use protection!'

Grabbing her new friend by the hand, Dawn's cheeks flush violently as he leads her out onto the street. Watching her walk away, I smile to myself as I see her apologising profusely for Gina's crude behaviour. After her disastrous last relationship, I really hope this goes well for her. Hugh might not be Dawn's Mr Right, but sometimes Mr Right Now is all that you need…

Chapter 6

Watching the world whizz by the window, I flip down the visor and check my teeth for sunflower seeds. We must have been driving for well over an hour and for at least forty minutes of that I've been eating my weight in glorified rabbit food. We ate a huge cooked breakfast before we left the house earlier, so I can't possibly be hungry. I guess I just need something to distract myself from the two terrors in the back. A road trip with a hyper three-year-old and an outspoken pensioner sounded a lot easier on paper. Picking a black pip out of my back molar, I dig out my iPhone and scan my notifications for any news from Dawn. Ever since we waved her off last night, I've been just itching to find out how it went. To be honest, I did expect to have heard from her by now, but I guess no news is good news.

'Are we there yet?' Noah asks, for what seems like the hundredth time.

'No, Noah.' Pulling my handbag onto my lap, I swap my handset for a lip balm and flash him a smile.

Frowning in response, he folds his little arms and scowls. I cannot tell you how many times I have seen that tiny angry face lately. Trying not to laugh, I bite my lip and turn my attention to the road ahead. As it usually is on a Saturday, the motorway is chaotic, to say the least. If only we didn't have to wait around for Janie to decide which vulgar and inappropriate outfit to wear this morning, we would have been there already.

'Are we there yet, Daddy?' Noah leans forward and hits Oliver on the head with his book.

'Not yet, buddy.' Oliver indicates right and swings around the roundabout. 'We won't be too long though.'

Straining my neck, I look back at Noah and smile fondly. His floppy curls hang in front of his huge eyes, just like Oliver's. I swear he gets more and more like his dad every single day. As much as I hate to admit it, any trace of me has long since vanished and all that remains is a mini Oliver Morgan. Not that I am complaining, I don't think he could have turned out more perfect if I tried. Looking at him now in his denim dungarees and checked shirt, I almost can't believe that I made something so damn beautiful. Abandoning his action figure, he sticks a little finger up his nose and proceeds to wipe it on his jeans. Yes, definitely all Oliver.

Applying a layer of lip balm, I scour through the pamphlets in my lap and start to feel excited. Oliver and I have wanted to take Noah to Virtuoso for so long and now he is *finally* old enough to appreciate everything that it has to offer. From discovering how human bodies work to learning how to fly in the gravity-free zone, it really is the perfect educational trip. Unlike most theme parks, Virtuoso incorporates learning and makes it fun. Pretty genius if you ask me.

'I still don't know why we're going to this stupid place.' Janie grumbles like a sulky adolescent and kicks my seat.

'It's not stupid!' I fire back, instantly feeling annoyed. 'I think you will find that it's informative and entertaining, actually.'

'Since when were *informative* and *entertaining* used in the same sentence?' She rolls her eyes and yawns loudly, making her disdain at being dragged along today clear to see.

Not wanting to lose my temper with her before we have even arrived, I glower at Oliver and send him a mental SOS to sort out his infuriating mother. Adjusting the rear-view mirror, Oliver turns down the radio and puts on his most cheerful voice.

'Come on, Mom! It's going to be great. I promise!'

Not bothering to answer him with more than a grunt, Janie attempts to pull her taut brow into a frown. I'm about to tell her that the downside of five face-lifts is that you permanently have the expression of a surprised mannequin when Noah taps my shoulder again.

'Are we there yet?' He sings loudly. 'Are we there yet? Are we there yet? Are we there yet?'

'Not yet.' I shake my head and hand him his portable DVD player in the hope that it keeps him quiet for a while.

Carefully taking it from me, he jabs at the screen and settles down in his seat. Thank God for that! When we planned this trip, I totally underestimated just how many activities I needed to bring to occupy Noah. Two hours is a breeze for us boring adults, but when you're a young boy it's not so easy.

'What are you watching on there?' Janie asks, leaning across the seat and ruffling Noah's hair.

'Dory!' He whispers excitedly, turning the screen so that she can see.

'Again?' Rolling her eyes, Janie puts down the passenger window, causing my hair to blow around like a rag doll. 'If I have to see that damn blue fish one more time, I'm gonna lose my mind.'

Desperately trying to keep my hair in place, I hold down my curls and strain my neck to face her. 'Can you put the window up, please?'

Choosing to ignore me, she sticks her head out of the window and hollers loudly, causing other drivers to give us some quite peculiar looks. What the hell is she *doing?* She's like the modern-day Benjamin bloody Button, retreating further and further into childhood the older she gets. Hoping that a hole forms in the ground and swallows me up, I grab a hair tie from the glove box and attempt to gather my locks into something that resembles a ballerina bun.

'Mummy, are we there yet?' Noah moans again, even louder than the last time.

Letting out an exasperated sigh, I rub my throbbing temples.

'Noah, if the wheels are still moving we are *not* there yet, OK?'

He looks at me intently for a moment, as though carefully processing this piece of information. I shouldn't really be getting annoyed with him. This car journey is starting to drive *me* insane, so I can only imagine how agitated he must be. Three-years-old and cooped up in the back of a Range Rover with his crazy grandmother. At least I have the comfort of being in the front with Oliver, I think I would have thrown myself out onto the motorway by now if I were back there with Janie.

Suddenly deciding that she's had enough of making a complete fool of herself, Janie closes the window and lets out a rather unladylike hoot. Obviously not realising that she has made her ridiculous beehive even more preposterous, she pulls down her shirt to ensure that she's revealing as much cleavage as possible. For a moment I debate telling her, before deciding to keep shtum. Let's face it, she certainly wouldn't tell me if I was rocking a hairstyle last seen on Cyndi Lauper circa 1984.

We approach a set of traffic lights and I notice a sign which states Virtuoso. Breathing a sigh of relief that we are finally getting close, I wiggle my toes to get some feeling back into my numb feet. Jeez, you know you're getting old when you can't do a car journey without worrying about your blood circulation.

'Mummy, are we there yet?' Noah trills, hitting me on the head playfully.

'No!' I yell, a little louder than I mean to. 'What did I *just* tell you? If the wheels are still moving, we aren't there!'

Erupting into a fit of giggles, he points out of the window and laughs. 'But the wheels aren't moving.'

Pursing my lips, I have to admit that he's got me hook, line and sinker.

'Mommy's not as clever as she thinks she is, is she, Noah?' Janie leans over and pulls out my hair tie, making my hair look almost as outlandish as hers.

Resisting the urge to give her a swift dig, I look over at Oliver for help.

'Well, if it settles your argument, I can confirm that we shall be there in exactly three minutes.' Oliver squints at the TomTom and changes lane.

A cheer erupts from the backseats and I can't help but smile as Noah claps his hands together happily.

'They better have a bar in this damn place.' Janie grunts, snatching the pamphlet from the armrest.

I'm about to add that I very much doubt a children's activity centre will serve alcohol when she lets out a sneer.

'*Visit our new biology centre and see what life is like inside the womb!*' Janie puts down the leaflet and pulls a repulsed face. 'Seriously? Why the hell would anyone want to do that crap?'

'Crap!' Noah repeats aimlessly, not really understanding what this word means. 'Crap! Crap! Crap!'

I take a sharp intake of breath as my blood runs cold. 'Noah!' I hiss, shaking my head. 'Do *not* say that word!'

'Why?' He asks, suddenly getting a case of the hysterics. 'Why can't I say crap?'

'*Noah!*' Oliver adds more sternly. 'Listen to your mother.'

Before I have the chance to explode at Janie, we pass under an enormous archway and come to a stop in the world's biggest car park. Immediately unbuckling his seatbelt, Noah huffs and puffs as he waits for Oliver to let him out of the car. Gathering my belongings, I flip up the visor and swing open the passenger door. Leaving Oliver to get Noah, I pop the boot and pull out Noah's buggy. As Oliver heads off towards the entrance with Noah on his shoulders, I reach out and jab Janie in the ribs.

'How many times have I told you not to swear in front of my son?' I attempt to keep my voice down as to not attract the attention of the other visitors, but I can feel my blood pressure rising with each breath that I take. 'Are you listening to me?'

Janie adjusts her bra, which is clearly two sizes too small and laughs cockily. 'What the hell are you talking about now?'

'Don't play stupid. You know very well what I am talking about.' A couple pull-up next to us and exchange worried glances before deciding to choose another parking space. 'I mean it, Janie. Do *not* swear in front of Noah again.'

'*Crap!*' Noah yells in the distance, sticking his tongue out from the safety of Oliver's shoulders and laughing.

Janie clasps her hand to her mouth and joins in with his laughter.

'Are you for real?' I seethe, not knowing whether to laugh or cry. 'What kind of person finds a three-year-old swearing humorous?'

'It was a slip of the tongue, Clara and besides, *crap* is hardly a curse word.' Her tone of voice indicates that she thinks I'm over-reacting, which just makes me even angrier.

'Crap most certainly *is* a curse word!' I shout, feeling my heart pound in my chest. 'Especially when it comes out of the mouth of a three-year-old, *my* three-year-old!'

'Alright! Alright!' Holding up her hands to surrender, she reaches out and claps me on the back. 'I'm sorry, alright? Do you forgive me?'

Not being prepared to drop the subject so easily, I look down at the ground and try to calm my breathing. Not only does this woman drink a bottle of bourbon a day, but she has now crossed the line into passing her potty mouth on to my child. How much more of this am I supposed to take?

Shaking my head, I give her a final scowl before heading off in search of Oliver. Despite my efforts to keep our heated discussion discreet, a few of the other visitors are giving me cautious glances, obviously having overheard our fiery exchange. Trying to avoid eye contact, I weave my way through the sea of people in search of Oliver. With him clearing six feet tall, he's always fairly easy to spot in a crowd and after a few minutes of scouring the area, I finally locate him by the ticket office.

Secretly hoping that I've lost Janie in the swarms of people, I come to a stop next to Oliver and tap him on the arm.

'Have you paid?' I ask, stepping to the side to avoid losing my toes to an antsy wheelchair user.

'Yeah.' Oliver nods in response and hands me a pale blue stub. 'Where's my mom? If we lose her in here, we'll never find her.'

'We should be so lucky.' I mumble under my breath.

'What was that?' Oliver leans closer and frowns.

'I said, *she'll find us.*' Pushing him towards the turnstiles, I tell myself to forget about Janie and start enjoying myself. 'Come on, let's go.'

Following him along the lobby, I dig my pamphlet out of my back pocket and squint at the tiny map. The last time we went to an amusement park like this was in Florida last year. A frisson of annoyance washes over me as I recall the chaos that Janie caused on that trip, too. She's like a bloody hurricane, causing destruction wherever she goes before moving on to a new destination. Holding on to the hope that she will soon be someone else's rainy day, I look up at Oliver and point at the sign overhead.

'How about we start at the Fly Zone?' I hand him the pamphlet and take Noah by the hand.

'Sounds good to me.' He nods in agreement and scans the crowd behind us. 'Let me just go and find my mom and we'll head straight for it.'

Letting out an inward groan, I pray that he doesn't find her and wander along the hallway. The stream of children running past disappear into the Insect Village, leaving just Noah, I and a few elderly members of staff. Deciding to take the opportunity to tell him just how bad Janie's language is, I crouch down to his level and look at him sternly.

'Noah, that word you said before was very naughty. Do you know which word I am talking about?' I am trying to be diplomatic, but I can tell from the cheeky look on his face that he isn't taking this conversation seriously.

Noah nods and beams back at me, cupping his hands around his mouth. '*Crap!*' He suddenly screams, so loud that it hurts my ears.

'Noah!' I yell, completely mortified. 'Don't you dare say...'

'Crap!' Jumping up and down on the spot, he sticks his tongue out and sings at the top of his voice. 'Crap! Crap! Crap! Cr...'

Clamping my hand over his mouth, I feel my cheeks flush violently as I try desperately to stop him from shouting. The elderly ladies behind us gasp and shoot me filthy looks. Resorting to picking him up, I follow the signs for the toilets and run into a cubicle. To add insult to injury, someone has thrown toilet paper everywhere, so I sit him on my lap and hold both of his hands in mine.

'Noah, if you say that word *one* more time...'

'Crap...' He mumbles, before suddenly looking rather guilty and frowning.

My jaw drops open as I stare at him in shock. What has happened to my gorgeous little baby? Six months of Janie has turned him into a complete devil. What will the next six months bring? Drugs and tattoos? She has to go! Hearing someone close the door on the cubicle next to mine, I close my eyes and lower my voice to a whisper.

'Swearing is bad. Very, *very* bad. It's so bad, that if Santa Claus hears you swearing, he won't bring you *any* Christmas gifts.'

Yes, I know, threatening my child with the possible absence of Santa probably isn't going to win me any Mother of the Year awards, but right now it's the best that I've got. Refusing to look at me, he sticks out his bottom lip and I know that I'm finally getting somewhere.

'Gee-Gee says it...' Playing with the hem of his shirt, he brings his eyes up to meet mine.

'Well, Gee-Gee is a very bad grandma.' I purse my lips and frown back at him.

'She is?' He asks, clearly a little shocked at someone daring to insult his beloved Gee-Gee.

'Yes, she is. I think I can safely say that Santa Claus won't be bringing Gee-Gee *anything* this year.'

Noah's mouth hangs open as he stares at me in disbelief. 'Won't Gee-Gee be sad?'

'Probably, but sad or not she's still getting a big fat nothing. Now, are you going to say *sorry* so that we can enjoy our day?'

Nodding furiously, he squeezes his hands out of my grasp and throws his arms around my neck.

'Sorry, Mummy.' He plants a wet kiss on my nose and squeezes tightly.

My heart fills with pride and I return his apology with a smile. Despite his moments of mischief, I can't stay mad at him for long. He flashes me those big eyes and all feelings of anger just melt away. Pulling open the lock, I lead him outside and squeeze by the line of children who are waiting to pee.

'Mummy?' Noah pulls me back as we step out into the lobby.

'Yes?'

'Now that I've said sorry, will Santa bring me presents at Christmas?'

Trying my hardest not to laugh, I nod slowly and swallow the giggle that is tickling my throat.

'Yes, Noah. I think he just might...'

Chapter 7

Peeling open my eyes, I stretch my arms over my head and let out a lazy yawn. Immediately noticing that I'm awake, Pumpkin jumps onto the bed and curls up next to Oliver. I run my fingers through her silky fur and smile as she automatically rolls onto her back. If heaven were a place, I am pretty sure this would be it. Well, this or a Caribbean beach with a Pina Colada. As you have probably guessed, it's Sunday, which is my second favourite day of the week. If I could wave a magic wand and make the week consist solely of Fridays and Sundays, I would do it in a heartbeat.

Rolling onto my side, I snuggle my nose into Oliver's back and allow my eyes to close. One of the best things about tiring Noah out is that he sleeps like a baby the following day, which allows Oliver and I to have a much-needed lie-in. Isn't it funny how once you become a parent, the best gift you could ever receive is a few extra hours of delicious sleep? When we first met, the *last* thing we would be doing in a plush bed like this would be sleeping. These days nothing turns us on more than the thought of a full eight hours sleep of a night, which is very rarely achieved.

After our rather action-filled day yesterday, this rare moment of peace is exactly what the doctor ordered. Apart from our very sour start, we actually had a lot of fun. I should probably clarify here that when I say *we,* I mean Oliver, Noah and I. Janie, on the other hand, spent the entire day complaining about the number of children and chatting up the many single dads who were clearly petrified of her. Due to the rather unfortunate swearing incident, I didn't so much as look in her direction for the rest of the day. On reflection, I think that's the only way I'm going to survive living with her. Pretending that she doesn't exist is a hell of a lot easier than trying to deal with the many, *many* problems that she brings. My mother taught me from a young age that ignorance is bliss, but I never thought I would be using that piece of advice to keep me out of prison.

Just as I am drifting off, my phone pings from the bedside table. Not wanting to wake Oliver, I roll over and feel around for the handset. I jab repeatedly at the screen until it springs to life, blinding me with a bright white light. The first thing I notice is that I have a text from Dawn. The second is that it contains the words *love*, *marriage* and *amazing*. Sitting bolt upright, I hold my breath and read the entire thing with bleary eyes.

Sorry I've not been in touch since Friday. I lost my phone once we left Artemis and I've only just managed to get a replacement sorted. Date was OK, not amazing and certainly not marriage material. I did have a lot to drink though, so I don't think he fell in love with me either! LOL.

Sliding back under the sheets, I can't help but feel deflated. I know it was unlikely, but the lack of contact from her made me think that she was wrapped up with the gorgeous stranger in a luxury hotel room, surrounded by empty wine bottles and discarded clothing. I did pass this fantasy onto Gina who said there was more chance of her being locked in a basement somewhere being force-fed tinned beans. Trust Gina, always the optimist.

Sliding my phone under the pillow, I realise that I'm not going to be able to fall back asleep and grab my dressing gown from the back of the door. A quick glance at my watch tells me that it's almost 10am and I am suddenly a little concerned as to why Noah hasn't come running into our room yet. Motioning for Pumpkin to follow me, I wander across the living room and throw open the balcony doors. Leaving her to use the facilities, I pad into Noah's room and have a mini panic attack when I realise that he isn't in his bed.

'Noah?' I yell, scanning his room with eyes like saucers. 'Noah?'

'He's in here!' Janie's familiar voice leads me into the spare room and I allow myself to breathe again.

'There you are!' I sigh, clasping my hands to my chest dramatically as I find Noah cross-legged on the end of Janie's bed.

'Where the hell did you think he was?' Janie looks up from her magazine and shakes her head. 'Looking for hookers in Covent Garden?'

'Janie!' I shoot her a deathly glare and pull my dressing gown tightly around my body. 'Please refrain from associating my son with hookers, thank you very much.'

Looking around the room, I can't help but frown as I take in the mess that is strewn around our spare bedroom. She really is a slob. How someone can spend so long on their appearance, but live like a homeless hobo is beyond me. Creeping past the dirty laundry and discarded anti-ageing products, I make my way over to Noah and perch on the bed next to him. Totally engrossed in whatever it is that he's playing with, he doesn't even bother to look up.

'What have you got there?' I ask, suddenly aware of a strange buzzing sound. 'Is there a fly in here?'

'It's not a fly, silly!' Noah shakes his head and giggles, causing his curls to flop in front of his eyes. 'It's Gee-Gee's bunny!'

'Bunny?' I screw up my nose and look at Janie, wondering what he's talking about. 'What bunny?'

Turning around to face me, he holds up a bright pink and extremely large...

'Look, it tickles!' Holding it on the tip of his nose, he squeals like a piglet and collapses into hysterics.

Oh, God! Bile rises in my throat as I wrestle with Noah for the rabbit inspired vibrator. 'Noah, give it to me!' My voice is shrill with shock as I attempt to take it from him.

'No!' He bats my hands away frantically and buries it beneath the sheets.

'Give it to me!' I shriek, throwing around the bedding like a prison inspector.

His face turns red with anger as he tries his best to keep his new toy hidden from his mean mum.

'Noah!' My heart pounds in my ears and I bang my hand down on the mattress. 'Drop it this *instant!*'

Looking absolutely petrified, Noah hands me the offending object and immediately bursts into tears.

'Why are you shouting at me?' He wails, throwing himself down on the bed. 'I was just playing!'

Taking Noah by the hand, I storm out of the room and plonk him in front of the television, which as usual silences him in a nanosecond. I actually do *not* believe what I have just witnessed in there. I feel like I should be drenching Noah in disinfectant and putting him through a boil wash. That's it. I am sick to the back teeth of this vile excuse for a mother-in-law and her frankly disgusting behaviour. This time she's gone too far. Marching back into her room, I kick the door shut and try to stop my hands from shaking. Picking up the vibrator with the tips of my fingers, I launch it at Janie and silently cheer as it lands on her head with a thud.

'Oww! What the hell are you doing?' She yells, finally tearing herself away from her gossip magazine. 'What was that for?'

'Are you kidding me?' I hiss, taking a few steps towards her. 'You gave my son a *vibrator* to play with? What the hell is wrong with you?'

'Jesus Christ!' Tossing her magazine onto the floor, she throws her legs over the edge of the bed and pushes herself to her feet. 'Will you relax?'

'Relax?' I screech, suddenly worried that my head might actually explode. 'Do *not* tell me to relax!'

Janie looks at me as though I have lost my mind and tosses me an empty black box. 'It was brand new in the packaging! He stumbled across it looking for his cars. He doesn't know what it is. To Noah, it's just another toy!'

Now it's my turn to look bewildered. 'I don't *care* what he thought it was! It's unhygienic and perverted!'

'Did you not listen to a word I've just said? It was *new in the box!*' Janie folds her arms and scowls. 'It was easier to let him play with it than have him scream the goddam apartment down.'

My bottom lip trembles with anger and I fight against it. For six months, I've been keeping my rage bottled up and not saying anything for fear of upsetting Oliver, but I can't keep it in any longer. I am going to explode. Like a can of Pepsi Max that has been shaken furiously for weeks on end, I am going to erupt into a fizzy volcano. Taking a step towards her, I rest my hands on my hips and take a deep breath.

'Janie...'

'What's going on in here?' Oliver pops his head around the door and frowns sleepily. 'Noah said you shouted at him about a rabbit or something?'

Spinning around, I feel frozen to the spot as he waits for me to respond. Not wanting to tell him that I was about to karate chop his mother because I just found Noah shoving her vibrator up his nose, I choose to say nothing and push past him.

Storming into the kitchen, I flip open the bread bin and drop two slices into the toaster. My heart is racing and if my head pounded any harder, I am pretty sure that the vein on the side of my head would actually burst. Pumpkin scratches at the patio doors and I abandon the breakfast to let her back inside. As usual, her tail wags uncontrollably as she runs into the living room and plonks herself down next to Noah. My fury subsides a little as I watch the two of them together. Snuggling up in front of the television, they couldn't look any cuter if they tried.

Smoke starts to drift out of the toaster and I dash back into the kitchen just in time to save Noah's breakfast. Reaching for the jam from the overhead cabinet, I look up as Oliver comes out of the spare room, quickly followed by Janie.

'Whatever you're making, can I have some?' He asks, coming into the kitchen and wrapping his arms around my waist.

Wriggling out of his grip, I nod in response and proceed to cut Noah's toast into tiny squares. He plants a kiss on my forehead and flicks on the coffee maker before grabbing Noah and curling up on the couch. Brazen as ever, Janie strolls across the lounge and drapes herself over an armchair. Totally ignorant to the blazing row we have just had, she lets out a yawn and looks over in my direction.

'Any chance of a coffee?' She drawls, sprawling out like an overgrown toddler. 'And make it Irish.'

'Don't you think it's a little early?' Oliver muses, throwing Noah in the air and wrestling off Pumpkin who is trying to jump to his rescue.

'The sun's up, ain't it?' Letting out a hoot, she reaches down and throws a cushion at him playfully.

I don't believe this! Nothing, absolutely *nothing* that she does has a consequence. Where will this end? I swear, she could rob a bloody bank and still Oliver wouldn't bat an eyelid. I need to talk to him. I need to sit him down and tell him that *she has to go*. Listening to the two of them laugh and joke like they don't have a care in the world only adds to my frustrations. For someone who once branded England as cold, old and boring, she's certainly made herself very comfortable. Making a promise to myself that I will deal with this today, I place Noah's plate on the kitchen island and motion for him to come and get it. This needs sorting once and for all, because if she doesn't leave soon, *I'm* going to...

* * *

Leaning against the cold tiles, I look up at the shower head and enjoy the sensation of water running over my body. The strong pressure makes it almost like a massage as it pummels into my back. I inhale deeply as the tension that has been weighing heavily on my shoulders all day is literally washed away. Ever since the bunny debacle this morning, I've been itching to get Oliver alone so that I can tell him Janie has to leave. I came close on a few occasions, but between getting the grocery shopping and bathing Noah, there wasn't a single moment where we were alone together. Thankfully, the mother-in-law from hell decided to take herself out for a drink and now that Noah is snoozing in his bed, I finally have the perfect chance to tell Oliver how I feel.

Although I've made my mind up that I'm actually going to do this, my brain is going into overdrive thinking about what's going to happen next. I mean, as much as I want her to leave, where is she going to go? She no longer has a home in Texas to go back to and I know for a fact that she can't afford to rent in this neighbourhood. I know Oliver would help her out with money in a heartbeat, but I have an awful feeling he isn't going to want her to leave at all.

Tipping back my head, I exhale slowly and try to get my argument straight in my mind before I go back into the bedroom. There has to be a way of putting this so that he won't flip out or get his feelings hurt. As much as I can't stand to be around Janie anymore, at the end of the day she's still his mother and always will be, more's the pity. Shutting off the shower, I stick my arm over the screen and grab a towel from the rack. I'm about to reach for the toothpaste when I hear what sounds suspiciously like snoring coming from the bedroom. You have got to be kidding me! If he's fallen asleep after I have waited *all* day to talk to him, I am going to freak out.

Marching out of the bathroom, I push open the door to our room and come to a stop at the foot of the bed. Despite the Janie situation, what lies before me brings a smile to my face. Surprisingly, it's not Oliver who's making all the noise. It's a very cute, very tired Pumpkin who is stretched out on the sheets next to him. Her pink belly rises and falls with each snuffle that she makes. Oh, to be so gorgeous that even snoring just makes you cuter. Whoever said that diamonds are a girl's best friend clearly never had a dog.

'Have you heard this?' Oliver asks, grabbing his phone from the bedside table and hitting record. 'I've never heard her do that before!'

'Neither have I.' I reach down and stroke her tail, but she is so out of it that she doesn't even wake up.

As I watch Oliver snap away at Pumpkin, I decide that it's now or never to bring up the Janie card. Taking a seat at the dressing table, I fidget with the edge of my towel uncomfortably.

'Would you mind turning that off for a second?' I mumble, not wanting this conversation to be recorded. 'I want to talk to you about something.'

'Sure.' Jabbing at the screen, he rolls onto his side and tucks his arms under the pillow. 'What's up?'

'It's about your mum...' I manage a small smile and slide a little closer to him.

Oliver frowns and buries his head in the pillow. 'My mom? What's she done now?'

My mouth suddenly becomes insanely dry and I lick my lips frantically in an attempt to get my tongue to work. 'It's more what she *hasn't* done...'

'What she *hasn't* done?' He repeats, with a confused expression on his face. 'I don't understand?'

A wave of annoyance washes over me and I try to shake it off. Of course, he doesn't understand. Him understanding would mean that we wouldn't even be having this awkward conversation. Suddenly realising that this is going to be harder than I thought, I screw up my nose and sigh.

'Did you know that it has been more than six months since Janie came to live with us?' I look at him intently, hoping that he gets where I am going with this without me having to spell it out for him.

'Yeah...' He mumbles, turning down the television. 'And your point is?'

I purse my lips for a second, clearly sensing how this conversation is going to go. 'My *point* is that when we first discussed this, we agreed it would be a *temporary* arrangement.' Oliver doesn't say anything, so I carry on talking. 'Has she mentioned anything about, you know, *moving on* anytime soon?'

'What do you want me to do, Clara?' Oliver snaps, obviously getting agitated. 'Do you want me to throw her out onto the streets? Do you want me to tell her that you've had enough of her being here and that she has to leave?' His voice is low, but there is a sharp edge to it that makes me feel uneasy. 'You tell me, Clara. What is it that *you* want *me* to do?'

I scowl at the floor and shrug my shoulders. I knew this would happen. I *knew* it! This is exactly why I've been avoiding having this conversation for so bloody long. Pumpkin rolls over and skulks to the foot of the bed, clearly sensing that a row is on the horizon. Licking her paws, she tucks her tail under her legs and glances between the two of us cautiously. Suddenly feeling guilty that we have made her feel nervous, I lean down and scratch her ears.

I am about to give up and go back into the bathroom when Oliver mutters something under his breath.

'What was that?' I retort, not being able to stop myself.

Clearing his throat, he turns to face me and frowns. 'I said, *it would be different if it were your mom!*'

My skin prickles as I stare at him in shock. How dare he bring my mum into this! This is nothing to do with my mum! Unlike Janie, my mum would never put herself on us like this.

'Yes, Oliver, it *would* be different if it were my mum, because *my* mum would know when she had outstayed her welcome!'

My heart pounds in my chest as I pause for breath. We never argue, *never* and when we have a disagreement it's over something so minor that all is forgotten about five minutes later.

'I'm not having this conversation with you.' He shakes his head and rolls over to look at the wall, leaving me staring at his back in a fit of rage.

'Oliver, we have to talk about this.' Choosing to ignore me, he closes his eyes and hides his face in the duvet. 'Oliver, are you even listening to me?'

Not bothering to lift his head, he grunts loudly and sticks out an arm to shoo me away. 'I've just told you that I'm *not* having this conversation...'

'We *have* to!' Grabbing the duvet, I throw it back and hit him with a pillow. 'You need to understand that she's driving me insane! She is literally making me lose my mind! I can't take it anymore! I can't!'

He pushes himself into a sitting position and roughly brushes his hair out of his eyes. 'Don't be so dramatic, Clara. You don't want her here, I get it. You don't have to go overboard.'

'Dramatic?' I let out a scoff and throw my arms in the air. 'Most women would have had something to say about this *long* before now! Her behaviour is out of control! It's like she does it on purpose...'

'Oh, please!' He cuts me off abruptly and shakes his head. 'You're over-reacting, as always...'

My heart races as I stare at my husband in shock. This conversation is going from bad to worse! Not only are we arguing over Janie, now we are attacking each other.

'What exactly has she done that has bothered you so badly?' Oliver stares at me intently as he waits for a response. 'Well?'

Using a bobby pin to hold my towel up, I use my fingers to list all of the things that Janie has done lately. 'She rolls in drunk in the middle of the night. She leaves her junk all over the place like a scabby teenager. She teaches Noah curse words and last week, I caught her with a *man* in her room. I bet you didn't know that last one, did you?'

Oliver looks at me blankly for a moment, clearly disturbed at the thought of his mother doing it in our spare room.

'Did you just call my mom *scabby?*' Jumping to his feet, he swears through gritted teeth and grabs his dressing gown.

Not quite sure what to make of his reaction, I take a step towards him and scowl. 'Really? That's all you have to say about the fact that your mum has been having sex under our roof with strangers?'

Tying the belt around his waist, he swerves by me and pauses with his hand on the door handle. 'I'm finally getting close to my mom, Clara. After all these years, we're actually building a solid relationship. Why are you trying to ruin it?'

I open my mouth to speak, but he doesn't wait for my response. Watching him slip out into the living room, I stare at the closed door for what seems like an eternity before letting out a frustrated whimper. How did that escalate so quickly? A lump forms in my throat as I replay our argument over and over in my mind. He isn't oblivious to Janie's actions. He's deliberately ignoring them in order to build a friendship with his mum. Now I feel sad as well as angry. No matter how old Oliver gets, there will always be that little boy inside him who craves the attention from his mother that he missed out on as a child.

Feeling totally deflated, I flick off the light and crawl under the sheets. My head is racing and an overwhelming sensation of queasiness is making my body tingle all over. The last thing I wanted to achieve by bringing this up was to fall out with Oliver. Instead of taking a step forward and tackling this unbearable situation, I have somehow managed to take a big step back. My eyes start to fill with tears and I fight against it with everything that I have.

I know that everyone hates their mother-in-law, but I really did pull the short straw with Janie. Not wanting to allow myself to cry over her, I squeeze my eyes tightly shut and shuffle over to make room for Pumpkin. In an ideal world, Oliver would have said that he understands, and Janie would be searching for an apartment right now whilst I joyfully packed her bags. The reality is that I have just made things ten times worse than they were before.

Trying to stop my mind from going into overdrive, I resort to counting sheep in a desperate bid for some respite. I've moved on to silently singing the alphabet when I hear the door creep open and a strip of light flashes into the room. Oliver's distinct footsteps make their way around the side of the bed before I feel him slip under the sheets behind me. He doesn't say a word and neither do I, but the atmosphere is a hundred times lighter than it was just ten minutes ago. Not wanting to go to sleep on an argument, I roll over and snuggle my face into his back. Thankfully, he responds with a gentle squeeze of my arm.

'I'm sorry.' I whisper, feeling Pumpkin tuck in behind my legs. 'I didn't mean to lose my temper.'

'Me too.' He murmurs finally, before letting out a yawn and pulling the covers up to his chin.

Breathing a sigh of relief that we have made up so quickly, I find myself feeling hopeful that even though the situation blew up, I might have made some progress in making Oliver see that things *have* to change. Looking at the situation with my now very tired eyes, it was never going to be easy, but I am a big believer in that you can't have a rainbow without a little rain and dare I say it, the forecast is looking good...

Chapter 8

'Thank you so much, Mr Williams. I'm sure Sandra will love them.' I wipe my hands on my apron and brush a mound of soil from the countertop.

'Even more than the tulips?' He adjusts his braces and peeks down at the giant bouquet dubiously.

'Even more than the tulips.' I confirm, flashing him a reassuring grin and slamming the till shut. 'Have a great evening!'

'You too, Clara and thanks for, you know, everything...'

With a final grateful nod, he slips out onto the street and disappears into the crowd of people. Watching him go, I can't help but let out a giggle as I clear away the mountain of tissue paper. Mr Williams is probably one of my favourite customers. Without fail, he pays us a visit once a week. Each time with a different story about how his beloved Sandra is going to leave him. I've lost count of the number of times I have helped him to choose a suitable apology in the form of one bouquet or another. Weirdly, he has never actually said what the flowers are apologising for, but whatever it is, it only seems to get him out of trouble for a mere few days.

Tearing myself away from the window, I glance up at the clock on the wall and start to wonder where Dawn is. Eve doesn't exactly time our lunches, but two hours is pushing it even by her limits. To be fair, Dawn was met at midday by the hunky Hugh from Friday night and despite her initial reservations, she decided to let him take her out for lunch. It turns out that he was more infatuated with her than she was by him and after a bit of encouragement from myself and Eve, Dawn succumbed to his advances and off they went.

'Clara?' Eve's high-pitched voice trills out from the storeroom, causing me to lose my train of thought.

Popping my head around the door, I rest my hand on my hip and smile. 'What's up?'

Sitting at the computer with her secretary glasses perched on the tip of her nose, she looks strangely excited considering that she is doing the accounts.

'Is Dawn back yet?' She whispers, pushing her glasses up into her hair.

I shake my head in response and hope that she isn't going to get into trouble.

'Good!' Eve grins and closes down a spreadsheet. 'Go flip over the sign.'

'OK...' I reply uncertainly. 'May I ask why?'

Sliding off her stool, Eve tugs her Chanel handbag up onto the counter and shoves her arm inside. After a few seconds of rummaging, she produces a white bag and places it on the desk. The thin paper packaging means that I can already see what is inside.

'Will you do it with me?' She asks, holding out the pregnancy test with such hope in her eyes.

Not having the heart to decline, I give her arm a squeeze and head for the door. Please let this be positive. I don't think I can cope seeing her cry over yet another negative test. Saying a quick prayer, I switch the sign and slowly make my way back into the storeroom. Clearly not wanting to wait, Eve has already locked herself in the staff toilet and I can hear the tap being run at full pelt.

'You know... I really think it might have worked this time.' Eve yells above the sound of the water.

'Here's hoping.' I mumble, praying that she's right.

Hearing the toilet flush, I cross my fingers and paste a bright smile onto my face. Eve flashes me the thumbs-up sign as she throws open the door and holds out the stick. Not registering the fact that she has just peed on it, I accept the test from her and wince as a wet droplet lands on my thumb.

'Eww!' I whisper, dropping the test on the counter and frowning.

'It's just water!' Giggling like a teenager, she dries her hands on a paper towel and winks.

Not being entirely convinced, I reach for the antibacterial gel and try to refrain from looking at the result. This is always the worst part of these tests. Those agonising two minutes where you try to convince yourself that you aren't bothered, all the while knowing that you are. If you have ever taken a pregnancy test, you will know *exactly* what I mean.

'Did I tell you that I spent all weekend with a herbal doctor?' Eve muses, chewing the tip of her French manicure. 'She gave me so much fantastic advice and I've got this feeling that this could actually be it!'

I try to look positive, but a weekend of herbal healing isn't exactly giving me much confidence in the result. Checking the clock on the wall, I tap my foot as I realise it has been only thirty seconds. See what I mean about this being the longest two minutes in history? I glance at Eve out of the corner of my eye and feel a wave of sadness. This is absolutely heart-wrenching to witness. If there is any justice in the world, then a little blue line is going to appear in that little white window.

'Did you know?' Eve asks suddenly, hopping up onto the counter. 'When you took the pregnancy test for Noah, did you know that it was going to be positive?'

'Actually, I didn't.' I shake my head as I recall the moment that my life changed forever. 'It was Christmas morning and I was adamant that I wasn't pregnant, but Lianna literally forced me to take a test.'

'Christmas morning!' She gushes, clasping her hands over her heart. 'That's beautiful! Did your body fill with love the second that you found out?'

'Not exactly.' Shaking my head for a second time, I let out a laugh. 'I took so many tests before I finally allowed myself to believe it was real. It wasn't until my first scan that it really sunk in.' I look up to see Eve's eyes filling with what I hope are happy tears. 'Are you OK?' I ask, suddenly worried that I have upset her.

She nods in response and wipes beneath her eyes with her ring fingers. Reaching for a tissue, she glances up at the clock and lets out a squeal. 'It's time!'

I hold my breath as she takes a step towards the little white stick. It's hard to believe that something as insignificant as a piece of plastic is going to either make or break her.

'I can't look!' She sighs, covering her eyes with her hands. 'I really can't. You do it.'

Every muscle in my body freezes and I say a silent prayer under my breath. Please let it be positive. Please, please, please. My heart pounds in my chest as I slide the stick off the counter. As a child, I used to believe that if you wanted something enough and I mean really wanted it, then it would come true. Unfortunately for Eve, life doesn't work that way. Squinting at the tiny window, I stare at the vacant square for a good thirty seconds to make doubly sure before I speak.

'I'm so sorry, Eve...'

Her smile falters and she exhales loudly.

'OK... never mind.' Taking the test from me, she quickly wraps it in tissue and drops it into the bin. 'It's not like I haven't been here before, is it? Onwards and upwards.'

I smile sadly and stand back, watching her carefully. She took that a lot better than I thought she would. The last time we took a test together I almost had to call an ambulance she was that hysterical. I'm about to offer her a hug when she takes a seat at the computer and starts tapping away at the keys.

'Is that it?' I mumble cautiously. 'You're just going to go back to work?'

Eve takes her glasses out of her hair and pops them on. 'Not exactly...' Spinning around the computer screen, she grins and pulls me towards her. I frown in a desperate bid to read the text, cursing myself for leaving my reading glasses at home. Various profiles fill the page, each one detailing characteristics of the people behind the blurred images.

'Is that...'

'An egg bank.' She confirms proudly, pulling a notepad out of her apron pocket and pointing at a list of numbers.

I open my mouth to speak, but I'm not quite sure what it is that I want to say.

'Wow...' I manage eventually, looking between the screen and Eve and back again.

With Owen and Eve not being able to conceive after two years of trying, I was obviously aware that there was some kind of underlying medical issue, but Eve has never divulged exactly what that problem is. To see her looking at other women's eggs is actually quite a shock.

Obviously sensing my confusion, Eve purses her lips and fidgets with the sleeve of her shirt. 'Remember last week when I brought breakfast to the shop?'

'Yeah?' I nod along, wondering what on earth that has to do with Eve's infertility.

'Well, I wasn't just on a bagel run, I had actually been to a private fertility clinic on Smith Street.'

'OK...' A light switches on in my mind as I recall that day. 'I thought it was strange you were across town at that time in the morning.'

Eve laughs gently and shakes her head. 'I didn't say anything at the time as Owen really didn't want me to go.'

'Why didn't he want you to go?' I screw up my nose as I try to think of a reason as to why Owen wouldn't want to find out what is preventing them from having a baby.

'I dunno.' She exhales deeply and shrugs her shoulders. 'Male pride? Fear?'

I guess that makes sense. Acknowledging that you have a problem makes it all the more real. 'Does Owen know *now* that you went?'

'No. No one does. Just you...' She looks at me intently and I suddenly feel quite special.

'What did they say?' I ask cautiously, not quite sure that I want to know.

'They called yesterday with the results and it wasn't great, as I am sure you have guessed, but I'm relieved that I now know what the issue is.' Eve tears her eyes away from mine. 'After a few painful and pretty invasive tests, it turns out that I have PCOS and lazy ovaries, which means that there is a chance that I can conceive naturally, but that chance is slim. Very, very slim.'

'Oh, Eve...' My bottom lip starts to tremble as I realise that this probably isn't ever going to happen for her.

'No! Don't be sad, this is a *good* thing.' She reaches out and takes my hands in hers. 'After two years of trying, I *finally* have an answer to why it wasn't happening. Now I know, I can do something about it.'

I blink away my tears and put on a brave face. 'Well, yes, I suppose you're right.'

Sighing loudly, Eve looks down at her wedding rings and shakes her blonde locks. 'I really did think the herbal stuff would work, you know? I had this *feeling*, this *sensation* that it had done something, but clearly, I was wrong. However, it's not the end of the world as I have plan B.'

'And plan B is...'

'Eggs!' Eve yells suddenly, making me visibly jump. 'Do you want to help me find one? It's just like online shopping! Come on! It's so much fun.' Handing me the notebook, she pulls over another stool and passes me a pen. 'The first page are maybes. All of them are blonde-haired, blue-eyed, twenty-somethings in good health.'

'There must be a hundred names on this list.' I muse, scanning the lengthy numbers hesitantly. 'What does Owen think of this?'

'To be completely honest, he isn't bowled over with the idea. He thinks having a child that is half a total stranger is weird. He feels uncomfortable about it.'

'I guess I can understand that.' I look back down at the list and run my fingers over the pages. 'If it were me, I would always wonder what the person behind the egg was like. Do you know what I mean? I would want to thank the woman who had given me the gift of life. It's such a selfless and inspiring thing that these people do...'

Eve stares at me blankly and I curse myself for thinking out loud.

'I haven't thought about it like that before...' She mumbles, taking the notepad from me. 'I thought this website told me everything I needed to know, but maybe not.'

I chew the inside of my cheek and choose to say nothing for fear of putting my foot in it again.

'You don't think this is a bad idea, do you?' She whispers, closing the notepad and dropping it into her handbag.

'No!' I reply confidently. 'I think it's a *great* idea.'

'Really?' She murmurs. 'Now I'm not so sure...'

We sit in silence for a few moments and I find myself wishing there was something I could do to help her.

'If this is your only option to have a baby, Eve, I say you go for it. Who cares if you don't know the person behind the egg? Don't listen to me, you were right. Everything that you need to know is right there on the screen.'

She taps her nails on the keyboard for a moment and I can't help but notice her cheeks flush pink. 'Well, this isn't my *only* option...'

'It's not?' I reply, suddenly feeling optimistic. 'Then what's the second option?'

Eve stands to her feet and paces back and forth around the room. 'The doctor at the clinic said that if we didn't feel comfortable using a stranger as a donor, then we could use a friend or family member instead...'

I nod along, wondering if knowing your donor would make the situation easier or harder. 'That would be a big ask for someone though, wouldn't it?'

'It would.' She stops in her tracks and rests her hands on her hips. 'It would be a *huge* ask. There's probably only a handful of people in this world that I would do that for, you being one of them.'

Blood rushes to my face as I smile up at her. 'You're such a kind and generous person, Eve. You really are.'

'I'm sure you would do the same...' Eve looks at me hopefully and bites her bottom lip.

I open my mouth to speak and then close it again. Was that a rhetorical question?

'Well, I don't think... I mean, I'm not sure I could...' Suddenly getting a little hot under the collar, I lick my lips and take a deep breath. 'Eve, are you asking me to give you one of my eggs?'

'I am asking you to at least *think* about it?' She takes my arm and pulls me out of my seat.

'Erm...' Not having a clue what to say, I stare at my good friend as my heart beats rapidly.

'I understand that this is probably the biggest favour I could ever ask of you and I completely get it if the answer is *no*, but I want you to know that out of everyone in the entire world, *your* egg is the one that I would choose.'

She looks at me with such honesty in her eyes that I feel a lump form in the back of my throat. Feeling completely overwhelmed, I try to think about this clearly. 'What would that entail exactly?'

Jabbing at the computer screen, she clacks at the keys frantically before bringing up a webpage. 'From what I can gather, the procedure is pretty simple and straightforward...'

I frown at the screen as I take in a number of words that sound anything but *simple* and *straightforward*.

'I would carry the baby, of course, so it would purely be a case of firing out an egg and then Owen and I would do the rest.'

She is talking so animatedly that I can't gather my thoughts. I guess it sounds simple enough. A quick outpatient procedure and I can give Owen and Eve the gift of life. I mean, I'm not exactly thrilled about the idea of having a needle jabbed into my ovary, but what's a little pain in the grand scheme of things?

'No one would need to know, if you would prefer it to be that way, it could be our little secret.'

I nod in response and feel a frisson of excitement as I try to picture the prospect of giving my friend an actual baby. I could give them the final piece of the jigsaw that they have been yearning for so long. With one simple *yes* I could change their lives forever.

'You and Oliver have the most beautiful child in all the world. You're both healthy, you don't smoke, you're in good shape... and let's face it, you're both good to look at.'

I can't believe that I am actually contemplating doing this. What will Oliver say? Not being able to resist letting out a nervous giggle, I look down at my wedding ring and smile.

'What do you say?' Eve presses, clasping her hands to her cheeks and crossing her fingers. 'Will you be my chicken?'

Not wanting to commit to anything right now, I rub my face and exhale sharply. 'I'm going to need to think about it, is that OK?'

Her smile wavers a little, but she nods her head violently. 'Yes, of course, that is OK...' Furiously blinking back tears, she pastes a smile on her face as the door chime rings in the other room.

'So sorry I'm late!' Dawn's voice floats into the workshop and I position myself in front of the computer screen. 'You won't believe this, but I actually had a really good time!'

'Oh, we can believe it.' Spinning around, I smile as Dawn bustles her way into the storeroom with her arms laden with bags. 'What's with all the shopping?'

She dumps the mountain of plastic onto the floor and shakes off her coat. 'Hugh insisted on helping me to choose an outfit for Thursday. He's a buyer for Vision! Did I tell you that?'

'Only three times.' I exchange sideways glances with Eve and poke my nose into one of her bags before nodding approvingly. 'Very nice.'

'What's happening on Thursday night?' Eve asks, discreetly closing the internet tabs on the computer.

'Oh, erm... Hugh is taking me to the theatre.' She tries to say this as nonchalantly as possible, but no matter how hard she tries she can't stop her cheeks from flushing pink.

'Aren't you working Thursday afternoon?' Eve muses, flipping through the rota on her desk.

'Oh, sugar...' Dawn leans against the wall and sighs. 'I completely forgot.'

Eve taps her pen on the rota, clearly trying to juggle things around so that Dawn can go to the ball. Deciding to take one for the team, I roll my eyes and turn to face Eve.

'I'll cover for her.'

'You will?' Dawn squeals loudly and claps her hands together.

'I will.'

'Thank you! Thank you! Thank you!' Throwing her arms around my neck, she buries her face in my hair and smothers me in kisses. 'You're a superstar!'

Fighting her hair out of my mouth, I look over my shoulder at Eve and wink.

'Well, what are friends for?'

Chapter 9

Striding down the street, I wrap my scarf around my nose as the wind lashes against my face. What started as a bright and sunny day has unfortunately transpired into a pretty miserable evening. The sun is firmly shielded behind a mountain of grey cloud and even though the temperature is quite pleasant, there's a sharp backwind that is wickedly whipping through the air. Despite the terrible weather, I haven't been able to wipe the silly grin off my face all day. Ever since my conversation with Eve, I have been just itching to get home to Oliver so I can tell him all about it. He's going to be so made up, I just know it!

Feeling my mobile vibrate in my coat pocket, I stop in my tracks and jab at the screen. No doubt this is Eve with yet another quote about love, friendship and the beauty of giving. To be honest, I'm surprised Dawn hasn't clocked that something is going on between us. From giving me spontaneous back massages to offering up her last Rolo, Eve has made it quite clear that she is prepared to go to all lengths to get her hands on one, or as it turns out, a whole bunch of my eggs. Between managing a last-minute birthday party and batting away Eve, I managed to do a little bit of research on what exactly is involved with egg donation. I must admit that I was a little concerned when I realised there was a possibility of Eve having twins, triplets or even more. She may even end up with a whole football team, but hey, it's her funeral.

I shove my handset back into my pocket and continue on my journey when I spot a familiar head bobbing through the crowd. Quickening my pace, I haul my handbag up onto my shoulder as I come to a stop in front of the two faces that I know and love.

'What are you two doing here?' I ask, looking up at Oliver and smiling happily.

'We thought we would come and take you out for dinner, didn't we, Noah?' He glances down at Noah who is too consumed with his tablet to be bothered answering.

'Well, that's a nice surprise!' I gush, discreetly looking behind him for Janie and praying that she isn't here. 'Is it just the two of you?'

Oliver lets out a low laugh and nods. 'If you're talking about my mom, she's gone to meet Gina for dinner, so you're good.'

I sigh dramatically and flash him a wink before linking my arm through his. 'So, where am I being taken to, exactly?'

'That's Noah's decision.' Oliver tugs Noah's hood to get his attention and clears his throat. 'Where are we heading, buddy?'

'McDonald's.' He replies with a grin, before turning back to the tablet.

'McDonald's?' I repeat, glancing at Oliver doubtfully. 'Are you sure that's the best place to take your mom?'

'What do you think, buddy?' Oliver asks Noah, sensing my disappointment.

'Mmm...' Noah looks deep in thought for a moment. 'What about Burger King?' Realising that Burger King doesn't seem to please me either, he screws up his nose before his eyes light up with an idea. 'I know, Pizza Place!'

'There you go.' Oliver laughs and squeezes my hand. 'You've got three choices. What's it gonna be?'

Burgers, more burgers or pizza. Hardly gourmet delicacies, are they? I let out a groan as I remember that I have filet steak sitting in the refrigerator at home.

'I guess I will go for Pizza Place...' I say, attempting to smile.

'Pizza Place it is.' Oliver confirms, leaning down to ruffle Noah's hair.

Feeling a little bad that I am rubbishing what was supposed to be a nice surprise, I smile encouragingly at Noah. 'Pizza sounds good to me. Who needs steak and lobster when you can have cheesy garlic bread?'

Noah gives me a half look before letting out a *yes* and fist-pumping the air. He's been absolutely glued to that bloody thing since the day he got it. Sticking out his tongue, he presses animatedly at the screen and frowns.

'Oi, put that damn thing away now.' Reaching down for the tablet, Oliver tuts and shakes his head.

'But I'm winning!' Noah protests, holding it behind his back so he can't take it from him.

Oliver raises his eyebrows and mutters something under his breath that I'm glad Noah can't hear. 'That thing is going in the trash when we get back to the apartment.'

'No!' Noah yells loudly, causing people to stop and stare. 'It's my birthday present! You *can't* throw it away!'

Noah starts to wail and I try to reassure him that Oliver isn't going to toss his beloved tablet into the bin.

'Oliver!' I hiss. 'It's keeping him quiet, just leave him alone.'

Shooting me a glare, Oliver gives me a look that could melt stone and scowls. 'It's not good for him to be spending so much damn time on that thing!'

Telling him we will discuss Noah's screen time later, I let him lead the way into Pizza Place. The restaurant is fairly empty considering that it's dinner time and we get seated in no time at all. Still fixated on his game, Noah doesn't give the menu more than a quick glance before deciding that he wants a stuffed crust pizza with curly fries. Maybe Oliver's right, he's going to have square eyes at this rate. After a quick scan of the rather limited menu, I decide to go for the daily special and wait for the waitress to scribble down our order.

'This is nice.' I say, when we're finally alone again. 'What made you come and meet me?'

Oliver shakes off his jacket and shrugs his shoulders. 'I dunno. I guess after last night I thought we had some making up to do.'

I nod in agreement and finger the edge of the drinks menu. 'Yes, I suppose we do.'

He holds my gaze for a moment, only breaking away when the waitress places three glasses down in front of us. Thanking her for our drinks, I reach out and take a big gulp. I might complain about his childishness, his impatience and his obsession with football, but Oliver is always the first person to say *sorry* when he knows he has done something wrong. I've always admired that about him. His ability to swallow his pride and admit when he is to blame is what makes him so incredible. Not only is he incredibly handsome, he is also as honest and genuine as they come. Yes, I am a lucky, lucky lady.

'I am sorry that things got so out of hand last night.' I whisper, ensuring that Noah isn't listening. 'I didn't mean for things to get so, you know, *personal*.'

Nodding along, Oliver slurps on his straw and reaches over the table for my hand. My heart swells as he runs his thumb along my wrist affectionately. I knew that bringing up the Janie subject would be worth it in the long run. Like ripping off a plaster, quick and painless. Well, it hasn't exactly been painless, but you get the drift. Now we can move, put the Janie phase of our lives behind us and come out stronger at the other end.

'I'm sorry, too.' He leans back in his seat and breathes a sigh of relief. 'And I can't tell you how happy it makes me that you have come around to my way of thinking.'

I pause with my straw in my mouth, a frozen smile plastered on my face as I try to work out what he means. 'I'm sorry?'

'I know you are, and you don't need to keep saying it, because it's OK. I forgive you.' He laughs and gives Noah a high five as he declares that he has won once again.

Forgive me? What on earth have *I* done to require his forgiveness? 'No, I'm not *sorry*. I said I'm sorry as in, I don't understand...'

Now it's Oliver's turn to look confused. His brow creases into a frown as he twirls his straw around his glass. 'The argument with my mom? You said that you were sorry as you realised you were wrong and I accept your apology, so now we can put it behind us and move on.'

I let out a cough and splutter on my drink. 'No! That's not what happened at all! *You* apologised because *you* realised that *you* were wrong.'

Anger bubbles in the pit of my stomach as I look him straight in the eye. I actually don't believe this! All day I have been thinking that Oliver has finally seen Janie for what she is, but for some inexplicable reason, he has deemed *me* to be regretful of our argument rather than the other way around.

'Oliver, you know that Janie has to go, don't you?' My pulse beats loudly in my ears as I wait for him to respond.

He opens his mouth to speak, but he is interrupted by the return of our waitress. Choosing not to say anything until she leaves, I cut up Noah's pizza and wait for Oliver to break the silence. Quickly realising that he seems to be in a sulk, I decide to speak up.

'I mean it, Oliver...'

Dropping his pizza onto his plate with a clatter, he roughly wipes his mouth with a napkin and shakes his head. 'I'm not having this conversation with you again, Clara. This was wrapped up and finished last night.'

'Yes, you're right!' I exclaim, feeling my blood pressure rising. 'It was wrapped up and finished because *you* apologised!'

'No, *you* apologised!'

Noah looks up from his tablet and I can see that he's trying his hardest to pretend he isn't listening. Clearly sensing the same thing, Oliver fixes a smile to his face and pats Noah on the back.

'We'll talk about this later.'

I don't want to drop it so easily. I want to fight this with everything I've got because if Janie doesn't go soon, I am literally going to lose my mind, but Oliver's tone makes me think twice. Begrudgingly picking at my pizza, my mind flits to Eve and as mad as I am, I attempt to change the mood with a piece of good news.

'Anyway, I have something pretty exciting to tell you...'

'Oh, yeah?' Oliver squirts ketchup onto his fries and rolls up his sleeves, sounding less than interested.

'You know how Owen and Eve have been struggled to conceive?' He nods in response and takes a sip of his drink. 'Well, Eve has been to a fertility clinic and she is thinking of using an egg donor.'

'That's great.' He smiles genuinely and takes Noah's tablet from him. 'I'm happy for them. Seriously, that's fantastic news.'

'It's great, isn't it? And the best part is that she is going to use *my* egg to do it!' My skin prickles with excitement as I remember how Eve looked at me earlier.

Oliver's jaw drops open and he puts down his pizza for a second time. 'What the hell are you talking about?'

'She asked me! Of all the women in the world, she wants to use one of *my* eggs for the insemination!' Reaching for a napkin, I lick a dollop of barbecue sauce from the corner of my mouth. 'Isn't that incredible?'

Oliver looks at me as though I have completely lost my mind and I wonder what on earth is wrong with him now.

'What?' I snap, tiring of his grumpy attitude. 'What now?'

'There's absolutely no way that you are donating your eggs.' He snarls, sitting up straight in his seat.

'Why?' I fire back, not missing a beat.

'Why?' He growls. 'I shouldn't have to tell you why! One, because it's an invasive procedure. Two, because it will biologically be *your* child. And three, because there is no way you will be able to take a back seat and watch a child that is half *you* be raised by someone else.'

I blink repeatedly. He can't be serious! 'It wouldn't *be* my child. It would be *their* child.'

'It would be half you! Noah's sibling! How can you not see that?'

My heart pounds in my chest and I seem to lose the use of my tongue. This is *not* how I pictured this going. 'I would be giving them the opportunity to have a child of their own. This is my chance to actually make a difference to the world in a pretty huge way.'

Oliver looks down at his food for a moment before pushing the plate away from him. 'No.'

'No?' I repeat, trying to keep my voice down. 'What the hell do you mean, no?'

'I mean no, Clara! Hell no! You are not doing this!'

'It's *my* body. You can't stop me.'

'Well, you're *my* wife.' He pauses for breath and I can tell that he's just a few moments away from blowing his lid. 'You see those rings on your finger?' I look down and nod slowly. 'We're married. You can't make a decision like this without me. What if it were the other way around and it was Owen who needed a helping hand? How would you feel about that?'

'I would be totally fine with it.' I retort, very aware that people are starting to look over at our table.

'Really? You would be totally fine about Eve carrying a baby that had my DNA? A baby that would look like me? A baby that would look like Noah?'

My stomach flips and I tear my eyes away from his. I hate to admit it, but the thought of Eve raising a child that would have Oliver's genes *does* make me feel a little uneasy. I mean, would he develop feelings for this child? Would he develop feelings for Eve when he sees her raising it? My stomach churns as a wave of doubt washes over me.

'Doesn't sound so good now, does it?' Oliver shakes his head and takes a chip from Noah's plate.

I exhale loudly and hold my head in my hands, hating myself for questioning my decision. Suddenly losing my appetite, I force myself to smile at Noah who is munching away at his food. My heart swells with pride as I take in his beautiful face. Before I became a mother, I never believed that it could be possible to love someone so much. To love so deeply that you would do anything and everything to keep them safe is such a powerful and overwhelming thing. Is Oliver right? Would I feel the same surge of motherly love for Eve's child if I handed over my eggs? My shoulders start to feel inexplicably heavy as I picture myself telling Eve that I can't comply with her request. It would break her heart. She would be absolutely devastated.

On one hand, it seems so futile to deny Eve the chance of a child when I have thousands of eggs which will probably never be used. Although now that Oliver has made me look at the practicalities of Eve having a child that is biologically mine, I am starting to question whether this is something I could actually do. When push comes to shove, could I really give away an egg that might potentially become a child of my own? Right now, I really don't know...

Chapter 10

The walk home from the restaurant has been pretty uneventful. After our rather heated disagreement in Pizza Place, Oliver and I ate our meals in a rather uncomfortable silence. Thankfully, Noah was so consumed in his game that he hardly noticed our cross words and when he did, he found the fact that we were arguing over eggs frankly quite hilarious. The large glass of Rioja I inhaled over dinner has started to work its magic and I am starting to feel a tad better than I did a couple of hours ago. It's clear that Oliver and I have some issues to deal with and to be totally honest, I really don't know how we're going to resolve them. Even though I protested so much, I do understand that I can't really go against Oliver's wishes.

To donate my eggs to the Lakes when he feels so uncomfortable with it would be unfair of me, but right now the Janie situation is causing me more concern. I have tried asking him nicely. I have tried giving Janie the cold shoulder and I have tried screaming until my throat is sore. I'm afraid to admit that I am running out of cards to play. Apart from demanding that it is me or her, I don't really know what else I can do.

Leaving the boys to use the lift, I decide to take the stairs in a bid to work off the mountain of cheese I've consumed. As I march up the steps, I try to ignore the burning in my thighs and power on through. Talk about a rollercoaster of a day. I can't remember the last time I experienced this whirlwind of emotions in such a short space of time. I've been up and down more times than a damn yo-yo.

Coming to a stop at our floor, I hold on to the railing and pause for breath. Between kicking Janie into touch and telling Eve that I'm not going to be the one who gives her what her heart desires, I *have* to find some time to get my arse to the gym. I am talking myself out of liposuction when Noah appears in front of me.

'Jeez! What took you so long?' He sticks out his tongue and reaches up to tug open the door. 'A snail is faster than you!'

'Don't be cheeky.' I whisper, gasping for breath. 'And I think you will find that before *you* came along, I was in pretty good shape.'

Sticking out his tongue, he runs ahead and catches up with Oliver, who is busy trying to get his key in the door. As usual, Pumpkin's snout is the first thing we see. She whines happily as Noah embraces her in a huge bear hug, clearly ecstatic that her best friend is home. I let out a yawn and unzip my coat as I follow the pair of them inside. A trip to the gym might be edging its way up my to-do list, but right now there's a bubble bath with my name written all over it. Stripping off my coat, I hang it on the back of a chair and let out a sigh, hoping that Oliver won't protest at me having a little *me* time.

'I'll sort out Noah and Pumpkin.' Oliver mumbles, tossing his jacket onto the couch.

Taking that as my cue to escape, I nod in response and mouth *thank you* at him before disappearing into our bedroom. Dropping down onto the bed, I remove my jewellery and kick off my shoes. Without Janie here, the apartment is beautifully silent, a silence I've rarely heard since the day she arrived. I stretch out on the bed and savour the moment. Allowing myself a few wonderful minutes, I inhale deeply and feel my stomach rise and fall. This is how life used to be. Life before Janie seems so out of reach now, it's almost like it has been erased from my memory. Oh, what I would give to go back to the days when my biggest worry was my mother's latest inking.

Not bothering to reach for my dressing gown, I strip down to my knickers and head for the bathroom. Tearing out my hair clamp, I push open the door and let out an almighty scream. Sprawled out in my beloved bath with her spindly legs draped over the rim, Janie throws back what looks like my Champagne and flashes me a wink. Snatching a towel from the rack, I hold it against my body in horror as my heart pounds in my chest.

'What the hell are you doing?' I yell, not caring that the window is open, meaning that the rest of the apartment block will be able to hear me. 'Get out!' Pointing at the door, my bottom lip trembles with fury. 'I said get out! Now!'

Clearly finding my infuriated state amusing, Janie twirls her fingers around the stem of the glass and laughs. Her bronzed skin looks ridiculous against the white bubbles, which I can tell from across the room have come from my precious Jo Malone bath oils.

'I mean it, Janie.' I am so angry that despite my efforts to stop it, my voice begins to wobble. 'Get out right now.'

'Jeez! Who died and made you queen of the world?' Boldly pouring another glass, she pulls herself to her feet and stands up straight.

Not bothering to conceal her modesty, she brushes away the bubbles and walks straight past the towel rack completely naked. Over the years, I have become quite used to Janie's strange obsession with wearing little or no clothing, but I still don't want to see her over-inflated chest if I can help it.

'Would you mind covering yourself up?' I scowl and throw a dressing gown in her direction, which she lets fall straight to the floor. 'We don't all want to see your lady parts.'

'Well, why doesn't that surprise me?' She throws back her head and cackles. 'I suppose your vagina is made of flowers and rainbows, huh?'

Slamming the bathroom door shut behind her, I march over to the tub and yank the chain. For a moment, I contemplate letting it go, but a sudden rush of adrenaline takes over my body and I am powerless to stop it. Tying the towel in a tight knot around my body, I throw open the door and prepare myself for a fight. She's not getting away with it this time. Following the path of wet footprints across the carpet, I march out into the living room.

Thankfully, Janie is now wrapped up in Oliver's robe, but unbelievably she is *still* drinking my Champagne.

'Why were you in my bath?' I hiss, folding my arms angrily. 'Why were you in *my* bath when there's a perfectly good bath in your room?'

'Mine needed cleaning!' She protests, waving her arms around in that nonchalant manner that makes my blood boil.

'Then clean it!' I yell, my stomach churning with anger.

She rolls her eyes and I look over at Oliver for backup. Maddeningly, he just shrugs his shoulders and pretends to be captivated by Noah's tablet.

'I'm sensing that you're a little sensitive about your bath…' Janie giggles and drapes her bare legs over the arm of the chair.

'I'm not sensitive about my bath! I'm sensitive about my rude mother-in-law using it when she's already made a mess of my other bloody bathtub!'

Janie runs her fingers through her matted hair and frowns at her many split ends. 'Lighten up! It's just a bath!'

'It's just a bath.' Noah repeats from his position on the couch, looking at me as though I am a mental patient.

Oliver glances up and nods in agreement. They don't get it, do they? None of them understands how *difficult* this woman is to live with. Tears prick in the corners of my eyes as I turn on my heels and stomp back into the bedroom. I won't let myself cry in front of Noah, I won't. Dropping down onto the bed, I lean forward and hold my head in my hands. Why does she get to me so bloody much? No one else in the entire world makes me as angry as she does. It's her outrageousness, her complete and utter refusal to be a normal person. The way that she takes everything for granted and crosses the line every single day. She's like a naughty child, pushing the boundaries and waiting for a reaction. A wise man once told me that a bad attitude is like a flat tyre, you can't go anywhere until you change it. Ironically, Janie actually *isn't* going anywhere.

Pacing around the bedroom, my eyes land on the huge photo above our bed and I let out a sob. Lianna made this for me before she left for Barbados. We spent weeks rifling through my old memory boxes and photo albums. I still remember the moment she gave it to me as we waited for our ride to the airport. The pretty canvas is covered in a collage of one hundred snapshot images. Everything from our first night out together to my pregnancy pictures and wedding day photographs are compiled in a beautiful timeline. Lianna has created a vision of my life over the years and looking at it now, I don't think I know what the next pictures are going to be.

I know this is going to sound dramatic, but I can feel Oliver slipping away from me. I can see it every time we have a cross word about Janie. Every time I flash her a glare and every time that I dare to say something vaguely derogatory about his precious mother. Where has his sudden protective nature over Janie come from? I ask myself that question every single day and I still don't have an answer. I look down at my wedding ring and feel a fresh surge of determination. I'm not going to let Janie come between Oliver and I, at least, not without a fight. Pushing myself to my feet, I swap my towel for a pair of pyjamas and twist my hair up into a bun. My reflection stares back at me as I throw open the door once more, reminding me that my marriage is something worth fighting for.

Still sprawled across the armchair, Janie smiles up at me as though there hasn't been a cross word between us, only fuelling my fire.

'Janie, can I talk to you, please?' It takes everything I have to keep my voice light, but inside I am about thirty seconds from crumbling.

Oliver glances over and turns up the volume on the television, clearly sensing that all hell is about to break loose.

'Sure.' Handing me the now empty glass, she rolls out of the chair lazily and waits for me to speak.

'Not here.' I hiss, pushing her towards the spare bedroom. 'I want to talk to you alone.'

Not daring to look back at Oliver, I follow her inside and allow the door to slowly close behind me. Janie drops her towel and I shield my eyes as she tugs on a pair of hot pink and totally inappropriate pyjamas. This damn room is worse than I have ever seen it and it takes me a good few minutes to find a spot where I can stand and not be violated by her belongings.

'What is it that you wanna talk about?' Janie gives me a smile that says she knows exactly what I want to talk about, but she's going to enjoy playing with me first.

Taking a deep breath, I decide to stop beating around the bush and come straight out with it. 'Well, *this* for a start.' I motion to the pigsty that is surrounding me. 'Look at this place! It's an absolute mess!'

She casts her eyes over the room and gives me a swift nod in response. 'OK, then I'll clean it up.'

'You… you will?' I ask, a little shocked by her willingness to cooperate.

'Yeah.' She reaches down and grabs a pile of dirty laundry from the floor.

Shaking my head in an attempt to regain my train of thought, I bite my lip and watch in amazement as she gets to work at changing the bed.

'Why haven't you cleaned it up before now?'

Janie shrugs her shoulders and scans the room for fresh bedding. 'You've never asked me to.'

Passing her a new duvet set from the wardrobe, I rack my brains and try to recall the many times I have told her to sort out this mess. 'Well, I shouldn't have to ask you. You're a grown woman, you should just do it.'

She chuckles and studies a bottle of neon polish that falls out from her pillowcase. 'Clara, when have I *ever* been classed as a grown woman?'

Panic sets in when I realise that she's about to paint her nails on my Egyptian cotton sheets. Turning to face the window, I look down at the busy street below.

'It's not just the room, Janie. It's everything. You're rude, you swear in front of Noah, you bring random men here, you don't respect *anything* that I say...' My voice trails off as I hear a sudden squawk behind me.

'You're kidding, right?' She whispers, her face falling as she realises that I'm serious. 'Why didn't you say something before?'

My jaw drops open as I spin around to look at her. 'I've *tried* to say something! Come on, Janie. You know that you've crossed the line with me.'

'I *always* cross the line! That's who I *am*. You knew what I was like when you agreed to have me come live here.'

I pause for a moment, wondering if I am going to regret what I am about to say. 'That's the thing, I *didn't* agree to having you live with us.' Janie opens her mouth to speak, but my tongue seems to have a life of its own. 'What I did agree to was having you with us for a little while whilst you sorted yourself out. This was never supposed to be a permanent fixture.'

We stare at each other in an excruciating silence and I suddenly hate myself for ever starting this conversation.

'Are you saying that you want me to leave?' She murmurs, a look of devastation washing over her taut face. 'Where would I go?'

I bite my lip and start to feel incredibly guilty. 'I don't know, but you can't stay here forever. You know that, don't you?'

Janie collapses onto the bed and pulls the sheets over her legs. 'No, Clara. I did not know that. I did not know that at all.'

I rub my throbbing temples and close my eyes, not really knowing where to go from here. It's only when I force myself to open them again that I notice Janie has tugged her leopard print suitcase from beneath the bed. I am about to ask her what she is doing when the door squeaks open.

'What's going on in here?' Oliver asks, obviously annoyed at walking in on a scene similar to that of the other day. 'This is becoming something of a habit.'

'I'm packing.' Janie squeaks, picking up random thongs and tossing them into the suitcase.

'*What?*' Oliver looks at me furiously and reaches out for his mother's arm. 'Why?'

'Clara has made it quite clear that I have overstayed my welcome.' She shoots me a pitiful look and tugs up the straps on her camisole.

'Alright, this has gone far enough.' Oliver ushers Pumpkin out of the room and looks between the two of us. 'I'm going to put Noah to bed and then the three of us are going to sit down and talk this out.'

I screw up my nose and scowl, really not wanting to get into yet another argument. Hearing him inform

Noah that it's time for bed, I rub my face and try to avoid making eye contact with Janie. Confrontation has never been my strong point, especially when it involves the people that I love. No matter how much I rehearse it, I let my heart rule my head and keep my real opinions hidden, meaning that I am the one to lose out every single time. I am debating returning to my room to cry when Oliver pops his head around the door for a second time.

'Alright, get your butts out here.' He bangs his hand on the wall and motions for us to follow him.

Feeling like a naughty schoolgirl, I exhale sharply and give him a quick nod before following him into the kitchen. I notice that he's poured three drinks and I pull a glass towards me before taking a seat at the far end of the bar. Not wanting to look at Janie until I absolutely have to, I take a sip of wine and try to steady my breathing. I can already tell that I'm going to come off the bad guy in this. If Oliver tries to make me the villain in this piece, I am going to lose it. I sneak a peek at Janie, who is sitting on her stool with a little girl lost expression plastered on her face. She certainly didn't look like that when she was lay spread eagle in my free-standing bath.

'So, how are we going to do this?' Oliver sighs and swigs from his beer bottle. 'Do we need a *talking cushion* or are you two gonna be grown-ups?'

I look down at my feet and fiddle with the stem of my glass, secretly hoping that we do go with the *talking cushion* idea.

'We don't need a cushion.' Janie sniffs and throws back the contents of her glass in one gulp. 'Clara has made her feelings towards me staying here crystal clear...'

I roll my eyes and rest my elbows on the table. 'Janie, you must understand where I am coming from with this?'

'No, Clara. I don't understand. I don't understand at all.' She wipes a tear from her cheek and I try to work out if this is solely for Oliver's benefit. 'You told me to make myself at home and that's exactly what I did.'

I squint suspiciously at her and wonder if those are crocodile tears. 'I feel like I have been more than fair with you, Janie, but it's like you go out of your way to annoy me and despite what you say, I genuinely believe that you enjoy doing it.'

Janie scoffs as though this is the most outrageous thing she has ever heard. 'Well, I can assure you that most certainly is *not* the case.'

'You can't think that your behaviour has been acceptable?' Oliver kicks me under the table and I choose to ignore it. 'You tell me that swearing in front of Noah, bringing men here for God knows what and treating our home like some cheap hotel is OK and I won't say another word about it.'

'I've been through a pretty tough time, Clara.' She shakes her head and looks at Oliver with glassy eyes. 'I guess I have let my hair down a little, but that's only because of what happened to me...'

'What happened to you? People go through a lot worse than a bloody divorce, Janie. Isn't it about time that you moved on? I mean, it was you that orchestrated the damn divorce!'

'That doesn't mean that I'm not hurting about it!' She retorts, any sadness in her voice melting away.

'Well, you weren't hurting about it when you were cavorting around Orlando with a spotty teenager!'

'I'm gonna step in here and say that was a little harsh.' Oliver points his beer at me and frowns, evidently not happy at being reminded of his mother's infamous conquests.

'But it's true!' I protest, starting to feel like I am being ganged up on. 'This was a *temporary* arrangement, Janie...'

Her bottom lip trembles and I suddenly feel pretty bad. After all these months of pent up anger and frustration, you would think it would feel better to get things off my chest.

'I'm not saying that I haven't enjoyed having you here.' My cheeks colour up as I blatantly lie. 'I'm just concerned that in the time you have spent with us, you don't seem to have made any plans at all for your future.'

'She does have a point.' Oliver chips in, making my jaw drop open with shock. 'What *are* your plans for the future?'

I look at Janie with bated breath, praying to every known God that she wants to book the next flight back to America. Obviously caught off guard, she looks between Oliver and I cautiously. 'I guess I haven't put much thought into it...'

Oliver nods, looking deep in thought as he reaches down to stroke Pumpkin. 'That's understandable, but I do think Clara has raised a valid argument. We should start to formulate a plan to get you back on your feet.'

I let out a silent cheer and smile gratefully at my husband, relieved that we finally seem to be getting somewhere.

'Would you want to go back to Texas?' He presses, leaning back in his seat and studying Janie closely.

'You still have the money from the house sale to get yourself a place, don't you?'

I pinch my leg to stop myself from saying that if I know Janie like I think I do, she probably drank the proceeds from her house sale a *long* time ago.

Janie opens her mouth to speak before deciding that she needs some Dutch courage first. 'Can I have a refill?'

Janie flinches as Pumpkin brushes past her legs and motions to the bottle of wine on the table. Smiling at Oliver as he fills her glass to the top, she takes a massive gulp and places it back down gingerly.

'What if… what if I didn't *want* to go back to America?'

A gasp escapes my lips and I suddenly feel frozen to my seat. No! There's absolutely no chance in hell that she is going to worm her way into staying here permanently.

Oliver runs his fingers through his hair and yawns. 'Then I would need to speak to my lawyer.'

Janie twirls a strand of parched blonde hair around her finger and leans towards him. 'What do you mean?'

Panic starts running through my veins as the realisation of Janie staying in the UK hits me. This cannot be happening! Is having a monster-in-law that won't leave deemed an acceptable reason for a divorce? I should never have let her stay here, not even for one night.

'Well, there's the visa situation to start with. Right now, you're here under a tourist visa, so I would need to look into the legalities of getting you a permanent one.'

Feeling the need to put an end to this conversation before it gets out of hand, I take a gulp of wine and rap my knuckles on the table.

'Is it even possible for Janie to get a permanent visa at her age?' Janie shoots me daggers and I hold my hands up to protest my innocence. 'That was a genuine question, I'm not making a dig.'

Oliver raises his eyebrows as he runs his fingers up and down his glass. 'I'm not sure what the regulations are, but if my mom genuinely wants to stay in the UK, then I will find a way to make it work.'

Janie reaches over the table to give Oliver's arm a squeeze and I fidget in my seat uncomfortably. Not wanting to drift away from the subject in question, I clear my throat and try to get this back on track.

'Let's for argument's sake say that we *can* get you a visa, where do you see yourself living?'

'With you guys.' Janie grins and fills her glass with yet more wine.

Crossing his arms, Oliver pauses with an unreadable expression etched on his face. 'As much as I have enjoyed these past six months, I feel that you would really benefit from living alone for a little while, do you know what I'm saying?'

Janie gives him a look that says she most definitely does *not* know what he is saying.

'For the majority of your life, you have had someone to lean on. You were married to my dad for forty years. Have you ever been alone with your own company?' Not bothering to wait for her response, Oliver continues talking. 'I think it would be good for you to develop some independence.'

There *is* a God. Not wanting to speak for fear of bursting the bubble, I sit on my hands and watch the drama unfold. Janie looks down at her knees and shrugs her shoulders, clearly not sold on the idea of being given the boot. Deciding to back Oliver up, I take the bottle of wine and pour the remnants into Janie's once again empty glass.

'I think you would enjoy your own place, Janie. Just picture it, you wouldn't have me going on at you all the time about being tidy. You could bring people back and not have to worry about it. Oh, and you won't have Pumpkin hairs on all of your clothes, because we both know how much you hate that.'

Pumpkin lets out a huff and takes her fluffy butt over to the rug in the living room. I swear that dog understands *everything* we say.

'I think you're right.' Janie breathes quietly. 'Independence is something that I could do with before I end up a crinkly old lady…'

I resist the urge to tell her that she's already a crinkly old lady and nod along in agreement. 'Exactly! You're going to *love* living on your own, Janie. I just know it.'

She looks at me for a moment too long before sliding off her seat. 'That's settled then. I'm going to stay in London and live alone.'

I offer her a bright smile and breathe a sigh of relief. She's going! She's actually going! Not quite as far as Texas, but still, she's vacating my spare room and that's good enough for me. I can't believe that I held off having this conversation for so long. It just goes to show that if you can communicate with one another, you can resolve almost anything.

'I think I'm going to call it a night.' Janie mumbles, fiddling with her shorts. 'I'll see you guys in the morning.'

With a tiny smile, she turns on her heels and slowly walks over to her room, closing the door silently behind her. I am about to throw back the last of my wine when I realise that Janie has left hers on the table. In all the years I have known her, I don't think I've ever seen her leave a drink, not even a single drop. This is the woman who puts bourbon in her coffee of a morning for crying out loud. I glance at Oliver and notice that he's staring at the glass, too.

'I am *so* glad that we have finally dealt with this.' I reach over and plant a kiss on his cheek. 'I feel so much better, thank you.'

Oliver raises his eyebrows and lets out a sarcastic scoff. 'Well, I'm glad that someone feels good about this.'

For some inexplicable reason, the mood seems to have become quite sombre and I can't quite pinpoint when exactly things turned sour. Pushing himself to his feet, Oliver wanders over to the sink and looks out of the window. The room falls into an eerie silence and I suddenly feel a little uneasy.

'Is everything OK?' I ask, not really wanting to hear his answer. 'You seem a little... off.'

'I'm fine. Everything's fine.' Oliver scratches his beard and refuses to look at me, indicating that things are far from fine.

'OK...' I mumble, trying to work out where this conversation went so terribly wrong. 'It's just that...'

'Just drop it, Clara.' He turns to face me and throws his arms in the air. 'You got what you wanted. She's leaving, so can you just drop it, please?'

I stare at my husband in shock, really not liking his tone of voice. This was just as much his decision as it was mine! Why is he suddenly acting like this was all my doing?

'I'm going to bed.' He announces suddenly. 'It's been a long day.'

I nod in response and play with a strand of my hair, not wanting to say another word in case I anger him further. Hiding my face behind my hair, I watch him disappear into the bedroom. Obviously sensing the bad atmosphere, Pumpkin rolls over and follows him inside. Looking around the empty room, I don't really know what to do with myself. I should be on cloud nine. I should be literally swinging from the chandelier, but something doesn't feel quite right. Oliver's words ring in my ears as I take my glass and pour the remaining wine down the sink. *You got what you wanted*. I *have* got what I wanted, so why does it feel so wrong?

Chapter 11

Staring at my reflection in the mirror, I apply a quick layer of mascara and try to ignore the nagging feeling in the pit of my stomach that something isn't quite right. The bad atmosphere from last night continued right through until this morning and now that Oliver has left for work, I am feeling more alone than ever. Today was probably the first time in the history of our relationship that Oliver hasn't woken me with a kiss before he left for work. That might seem like an insignificant thing to you, but I can't shake the annoying voice in the back of my mind that tells me it's a sign of something much more.

With a final slick of lipstick, I flick off the light on my dresser and grab my handbag. Happily finishing up his breakfast, Noah takes a piece of toast and slips it under the table to a waiting Pumpkin who gobbles it up greedily.

'Noah.' I say sternly. 'What have I told you about feeding Pumpkin from the table?'

Widening his eyes, he shoves the last piece of bread into his mouth and shrugs his shoulders. 'That it's OK because dogs need breakfast too?'

I swallow a laugh and shake my head. '*Noah...*'

'Fine, I won't feed the dog anymore.' He holds up his hands to protest his innocence and jumps off the couch.

'That's a good boy.' I take the empty plate and motion for him to put his shoes on. 'Come on now, we are going to be late.'

Dumping the plate in the dishwasher, I glance at Janie's room and debate offering her a morning coffee. As happy as I am that she will be moving out in the not-so-distant future, I really don't want her to leave on a bad note. Knocking gently at the door, I press my ear against the frame and listen for any signs of life.

'What are you doing?' Noah asks, jumping in front of me with his backpack and coat on. 'Dad says it's rude to eavesdrop.'

My cheeks flush pink and I bite my lip in a bid to stop them from colouring up. 'I wasn't eavesdropping.'

Noah narrows his eyes suspiciously and folds his arms, in a pose reminiscent of his father. 'Then what *were* you doing?'

'Nothing!' I mutter, suddenly becoming quite flustered. 'Let's go.'

Ushering him towards the door, I take one final look at Janie's room before taking Noah by the hand and heading for the stairs.

'Alright, mister.' I hold his backpack and fix my face into what I hope is a serious expression. 'Today we are going to have a race and it's a race that you want to win, because the prize is frankly incredible.'

'It is?' He asks, looking up at me eagerly.

'It is.' I confirm. 'But you only find out what it is when you win. So, are you ready to run?'

He adjusts his backpack and places a trainer clad foot on the first step. 'I'm ready.'

Letting out a sharp whistle, I deliberately hang back as Noah sets off like a firework. When I proposed this race, I didn't actually have a prize in mind, I just wanted to cheer him up as I have a funny feeling that he can sense the atmosphere in the apartment, too.

My legs start to burn as I take off after him and I suddenly question my decision to run a marathon before I've had my morning bagel. Pausing for breath, I hold on to the railing and smile as I realise that despite his little legs, he's almost at the top. Finally reaching the last flight, I let out a fake groan as Noah squeals happily.

'I won!' He shouts, far too loudly considering that it's so early in the morning. 'I won! I won! I won!'

Panting like an OAP, I raise my hand for a high five as I hit the last step. 'You did! Well done!'

'What's my prize?' He squeals, jumping up and down on the spot. 'You said I couldn't know what it was until we got to the top.'

'Oh...' I rack my brains for a make-believe prize as we make our way over to Gina's apartment. 'Well, your prize for winning the race is one wish.'

'A wish?' His eyes glint excitedly as he stops in his tracks. 'A *real* wish?'

I nod in response and wait for him to start walking again.

'Can I make it now?' He whispers, looking around as though he wants to keep this a secret.

'You can, but make sure you really think about it, because you only get one.'

Noah stares at me for a moment, looking deep in thought. 'I wish that Gee-Gee didn't have to leave.'

My jaw drops open and I take a step towards him, thinking that I've misheard. 'You wish that Gee-Gee didn't have to leave?' I repeat nervously, hoping that he corrects me.

Noah nods and fumbles with his sleeve. 'I heard you and Dad telling Gee-Gee that she had to go, and I don't want her to go.' His little eyes momentarily fill with sadness and I feel a pang of guilt.

'Noah, you shouldn't have been listening to that. That was a grown-up conversation. You don't need to worry about things like that.' I crouch down to his level and try to look positive. 'Remember what you just said to me about eavesdropping…'

He twiddles his thumbs and frowns. 'Sometimes you don't mean to eavesdrop. Sometimes people just talk too loudly.'

A lump forms in the back of my throat and I try my hardest to swallow it. What have I done? In my haste to evict Janie from our apartment, I've managed to fall out with my husband and upset my beautiful little boy. Yes, I've got what I wanted, but at what cost?

'What's going on out here?' Gina's familiar voice pierces my thought bubble and I plaster a smile on my face.

'We were just having a race.' I let out a laugh and take Noah by the hand. 'You won, didn't you, Noah?'

'I did!' He exclaims, running towards Gina who gives him another high five.

'Wow! Well done! Why don't you go and tell Madison, MJ and Melrose?' She beams brightly at him as he squeezes past her and dashes into the house.

I am about to ask Gina how her day is going when Noah stops in his tracks and pops his head around the doorframe.

'Mummy, I still get my wish, right?'

My stomach flips as he looks at me closely. 'Of course, now go and play.'

Watching him disappear inside, I try to ignore the intense nausea that is running through my veins.

'What wish?' Gina whispers, fluffing up her hair so that her huge hoop earrings jangle loudly.

'Oh, it was just a game.' I laugh nervously and change the subject. 'Anyway, how are you doing? I feel like I haven't seen you for ages.'

Gina frowns and leans against the doorframe. 'Yeah, because Friday was such a *long* time ago...'

I hit myself on the head playfully and force out a giggle. 'I meant Marc! I haven't seen *Marc* for ages.'

'I guess it has been a while.' She nods along and runs a finger over her pink engagement ring. 'Leave it with me, I'll sort something out.'

Flashing her the thumbs-up sign, I haul my handbag up onto my shoulder and head back down the lobby.

'Oh, wait a minute.' Gina hollers after me. 'We'll all be together when Lianna arrives, won't we?'

I stop in my tracks and spin around. 'Yeah, but that's not for another week.'

Gina frowns and rests a hand on her hip. 'You didn't get the email?'

'No...' I'm actually ashamed to admit that I haven't even looked at my emails since yesterday morning, which for someone who checks their emails every few hours is a cardinal sin.

'Well, you'll be pleased to know that Lianna has changed her flights.' Gina frowns as Melrose runs up to the door with what looks like Nutella spread across her cheeks. 'They arrive in two days.'

'Two days!' A smile springs to my face and I feel my spirits instantly rise. 'That's fantastic! Do you know why they changed their dates?'

'I don't. The message was pretty blunt, to be honest, but it can only be a good thing, right?'

'Right.' I agree, glancing down at my watch and realising I'm now very late for work. 'Well, I better get going. Have fun with the kids!'

I give Gina a small smile and start to make way back to the stairs. With the strain of the Janie situation weighing heavily on my shoulders, I am probably only ten percent as excited about Lianna coming as I was last week.

'Clara?' Gina shouts, just as I reach the end of the hallway. 'Are you OK?'

Her green eyes burn into me, concern etched on her face. For a second I want to crumble. I want to tell her that I am most definitely not OK, that my husband hates me, and that Noah is *going* to hate me when he realises that I'm the one making his grandmother homeless. Fixing my face into yet another strained smile, I simply nod in response.

'I'm fine.'

If only that were the truth...

* * *

Despite knowing that I'm already late for work, I somehow manage to make myself even later. Intentionally walking at a snail's pace, it takes me twice as long as usual to reach the florist's. Regardless of how hard I tried to push it to the back of my mind, Noah's words have been buzzing in my ears since I left the apartment block. *I wish that Gee-Gee didn't have to leave.* My heart breaks every time I picture his little eyes filled with such hope. What kind of little boy wishes more than everything else in the world that his mother wouldn't make his grandmother leave? Not for a bicycle, not for a new football, but for his darling Gee-Gee not to be given her marching orders. A sad little boy, that's who.

I spot an elderly couple across the street and feel tears pricking at the corners of my eyes. Each one holding the hand of a tiny blonde girl, they count to three before swinging her in the air. I watch them burst into a fit of giggles as they pause for pictures before heading into a toy shop. Why can't Janie be like that? Why can't she just be a normal grandparent? Why does she have to dress like an aging porn star and act like one too? The most heartbreaking thing of all is that Noah loves Janie despite all of those things. He doesn't care what she wears, how untidy she is or how vulgar she can be. To him, she is just Gee-Gee. Plain and simple.

So consumed with my own thoughts, it takes me a minute to realise that Dawn is standing outside Floral Fizz and another few moments to recognise that the shutters are still down.

'What's going on?' I ask uncertainly, coming to a stop beside her. 'Where's Eve?'

'I don't know.' Dawn chews on the tip of her nail and scans the crowd of people for Eve's blonde bob. 'I must have called her a hundred times already, but there's no answer.'

Suddenly feeling a little uneasy, I look down at my watch and frown. In all the years I've known her, I don't think I can recall a single time where Eve has been late for *anything*. I dig my phone out of my pocket to try ringing her for myself when a familiar silver fox catches my eye. Fishing around in my handbag, I hand Dawn a set of keys and motion to the shop.

'You open up. I'm just going to... see to something.' Flashing her a grin, I tap her on the back and squeeze my way through the sea of buzzing people.

Call me crazy, but I swear I just saw Owen hovering around outside the jewellery store. With Owen being the typical workaholic business type, he wouldn't be out of the office at this time if his life depended on it. As I get closer, my jaw drops as I realise that the man smiling outside Tiffany's actually *is* Eve's hubby.

'Owen?' I tap him on the shoulder and smile as he spins around to face me. 'What are you doing here?'

'Clara!' His handsome face lights up as he scoops me into a huge bear hug. 'Just the person I wanted to see!'

Taken aback by his sudden show of affection, I squeeze him back and wonder what's going on.

'How are you?' He asks, finally putting me back down. 'How are you feeling?'

'I'm good.' I tuck my hair behind my ears and give him a quizzical look. 'And you?'

His eyes crinkle with happiness as he beams down at me. 'I'm brilliant. Everything is brilliant, thanks to you.'

I open my mouth to ask him what on earth he's talking about when Eve pushes her way out of the jewellery shop and throws her lithe arms around my neck. Struggling to breathe, I manage to escape her vice-like grip and take a step back.

'What's going on?' I gasp, standing to the side to allow a stream of suits to pass. 'You know it's almost 9.30am, don't you?'

Eve giggles and shakes her head. 'Oh, don't worry about the florist's! Come with me. I have something for you.'

Not knowing what else to do, I allow her to take me by the hand and lead me through the crowd. Coming to a stop at a remote coffee shop, Owen holds open the door and ushers the pair of us inside. He points to a secluded booth at the back of the café and strides confidently over to the counter. Feeling a little bewildered, I slide into the booth and rest my elbows on the table. My heart races as I wait for Owen to return with our drinks. Fortunately, I don't have much time to obsess over it, as thirty seconds later he reappears along with three steaming mugs.

'Thank you.' I slide one towards me and drop in a lump of sugar. 'This is... *nice* of you guys, but what's the occasion?'

Owen and Eve exchange bewildered glances before fixing their gaze on me.

'*You*, silly!' Eve exclaims, banging her hands down on the table. 'You're going to change our lives, Clara...'

'She's totally right.' Owen nods along and reaches out for my hand. 'You're our angel.'

My heart leaps into my mouth as I stare back at the two pairs of eyes that are looking at me with such awe. *Oh, no!* They think I'm giving them my eggs! After all the Janie drama, I haven't had the time to even *think* about Eve's request. My mind flits to my conversation with Oliver and I feel a thud in my stomach. *Could you really watch Eve bring up a child that was biologically yours?* I look at Eve and picture her with a bump. I picture her in the hospital, and I picture her with a baby in her arms. *My* baby. It would be *my* baby. I look into their eyes and remember when that person in my mind was me. The bump, the labour, that overwhelming surge of love you feel the second that you lay eyes on your child...

I can't do it. I can't. Oliver was right. He was *totally* right. I can't give them my eggs only to put them through the agony of wanting the baby when it arrives. I couldn't take that chance. I *can't* take that chance.

'Eve, I...'

Eve holds her finger in the air to silence me and lifts a small blue box out of her handbag. Sliding it across the table, she entwines her fingers with Owen's and waits with bated breath. I stare down at the iconic box in front of me and run my fingers over the delicate white ribbon.

'Open it...' She presses, her voice high with excitement.

Swallowing the lump in my throat, I pull at the ribbon and flip open the lid. A tear slips down my cheek as I take in the stunning necklace. A delicate angel wing pendant, covered in glittering diamonds stares up at me. Tracing my fingers along the gold chain, which is sparkling like crazy under the bright lights of the café, I let out a sob.

'I told you, you're our angel.' Owen whispers, his eyes suddenly glassing over.

Before I can stop it from happening, one tear turns into two and suddenly I am bawling like a baby.

'I'm sorry.' I wipe away my tears furiously and close the box. 'I can't accept this.'

'Are you kidding me?' Eve sighs and brushes away her own tears. 'You're giving us the gift of life. This is the *least* we can do.'

Shaking my head, I bury my face in my hands and sob uncontrollably. 'That's just it. I'm not.'

I cry for what feels like an eternity, only stopping when I have absolutely no tears left. When I finally dare to look up, Owen and Eve are staring at me with devastated expressions on their faces.

'I'm sorry. I really, really am.' My voice shakes as I look at my two close friends. 'I thought I could do it, I *really* did, but Oliver made me realise that I couldn't step back and pretend that he or she wasn't genetically mine…'

Eve dabs at her eyes with a napkin and wraps her arms around my shoulders. 'It's OK, Clara. I understand.'

Clinging on to her, I bury my face into her shoulder and let the tears roll down my cheeks. 'I'm so sorry. I can't even begin to tell you how sorry I am…'

Another pair of arms wrap around me and I look up to see Owen squeezing me tightly.

'Is everything alright?' A worried-looking waitress asks, clearly perturbed at the sight of three grown-ups crying in the back booth of her coffee shop.

Pulling myself together, I give her the thumbs-up sign and wipe my face, hoping that she leaves us alone. Waiting for the waitress to get out of earshot, Eve reaches into her handbag and passes me a tissue. I hold it over my eyes and try not to think about the state of my make-up. Once we have all composed ourselves, I look down into my coffee and take a deep breath.

'I wanted to do this for you guys so badly…'

'Really, you don't need to explain yourself, Clara.' Owen gives me a sad smile and rubs his right eye. 'We completely understand, don't we Eve?'

I look at my dear friend and feel a surge of guilt run through my veins. Her bottom lip trembles as she nods in agreement. 'Of course, I understand.'

I exhale deeply and tear my eyes away from hers. I feel awful, worse than awful. I feel horrendous. I feel like I have let them down and that is what hurts the most.

Owen clears his throat and takes a sip of his coffee. 'It was a huge, life-changing thing that we asked of you. We are just touched that you would even consider it.' Rubbing his temples, Owen puts his hand on Eve's. 'We just need to go back to the drawing board and check out our other options.'

'Exactly.' Eve attempts to smile and blinks back the tears. 'You can't be sad about something you never had, can you?'

I smile back at her and will the ground to swallow me up. This is unbearable. I don't think I've ever felt more useless in my entire life.

'Now, let's not have another word about it.' Owen picks up the menu and drops it on the table. 'Who's up for breakfast? They do a killer fry-up here.'

Eve takes a quick sip of her tea and pushes the cup away. 'I don't know about Clara, but I'm not that hungry.'

'Me neither.' I mumble, being very aware that my stomach is doing somersaults as we speak.

'Besides...' Eve adds. '*We* have a florist's to run and *you're* watching your cholesterol.'

'Well, I guess that's me told.' Owen rolls his eyes and shoots me a wink. 'You girls get yourself off to work. I'll order a fruit cup, I promise.'

Pushing out her chair, Eve kisses Owen on the forehead and grabs her handbag. Taking that as our cue to leave, I give Owen a quick squeeze and trail after Eve, trying desperately to act as though nothing has happened. As we walk back to the florist's, I rack my brains for something to say, anything to break the awkward silence between us. Despite my efforts, we make it back to the shop without saying a word. As Eve heads on inside, I hang back as I hear my name being shouted in the distance. Spinning around, I force myself to smile as I see Owen running along the street towards me.

Panting for breath, he leans against a lamppost and holds out the blue box. 'I still want you to have this...'

My eyes land on the blue jewellery box and I shake my head. 'Owen, I can't accept that.'

'Please, we bought it with you in mind.' He looks at me intently and his eyes crease into a sad smile. 'Please? Don't make me take it back.'

With a heavy heart, I give him a nod and slip it into my pocket. Not wanting to cry for a second time, I lean over and give him a quick hug before slipping inside the shop. If I didn't feel bad this morning, I sure do now. How many people can I manage to upset in a single day? This must be some kind of world record.

'Can you give me a hand here?' Dawn hollers over the ringing of the phone. 'I've had three internet orders already and Mr Williams has called twice.'

Snapping back into work mode, I dash into the storeroom and make a grab for the handset.

'Hello, Floral Fizz...'

I make a note of the order and hang up, all the while trying to ignore the fact that Eve is sitting at her desk looking like a lost sheep. Reaching into my pocket, my hand lands on the Tiffany box and my heart feels heavy once more. Not wanting to mention it again for fear of upsetting her, I shrug off my coat and reach for an apron.

'I think Dawn's a little busy out front…'

'That's fine.' Eve cuts me off with a smile and flicks on the computer screen. 'You go. I've got to sort out the rota.'

I nod in response and make my way to the door. 'Eve?' I whisper, making sure that Dawn can't hear. 'We are OK, aren't we?'

'Of course, we're OK. We are *more* than OK. The fact that you would even contemplate doing this for us means more than I could ever tell you.' Blowing me a kiss, she motions to the door. 'Now go and help Dawn, I heard Mr Williams has called and you know he likes to deal with you.'

I let out a laugh and dash out onto the shop floor before I burst into tears. Wiping my eyes, I force my lips into a professional smile.

'Alright.' I beam at the line of waiting people. 'Who's next?'

Chapter 12

Waving off the last customer of the day, I rest my head on the countertop and yawn loudly. In a frustrating turn of events, today has turned out to be the busiest day of the year. From a huge wedding booking to one too many guilty men seeking out the dreaded carnations, Dawn and I haven't stopped for hours. After the most heartbreaking and tear-jerking morning of my life, the highlight of the afternoon came in the form of Mr Williams. As usual, he required assistance in building the perfect bouquet for Sandra. This time we went for lilies, although it did take some convincing to persuade him that they weren't just for funerals. My skin tingles fondly as I picture him trundling up the street, briefcase in one hand, flowers in the other. Whoever Sandra is, she's a lucky lady.

Dawn jabs me in the ribs, effectively popping my thought bubble. 'What's going on with you and Eve?' She whispers, causing my blood to momentarily run cold.

'Nothing!' I stammer, pinging open the till and taking out the cash tray. 'What makes you think something is wrong?'

Dawn looks over her shoulder to make sure Eve is out of earshot. 'Oh, come off it! You haven't said more than two words to each other all day!' Dawn screws up her nose and frowns.

My brain goes into overdrive as I try to think of something that would explain our strange behaviour.

As much as I hate to admit it, there's been a prickly atmosphere between Eve and myself, despite her reassurances earlier.

'You're not ill, are you?' Dawn's expression suddenly changes and she pulls me closer to her. 'You *would* tell me, wouldn't you?'

'No!' I hiss, mortified that Dawn would think I'm on my way out. 'Not at all. I promise you it's nothing like that.'

She squints suspiciously and studies my face. 'Then what is it?'

I exhale sharply and strip off my apron. I really don't think it's my place to tell Dawn about Eve's proposal, but I don't want her to jump to the wrong conclusion either. The lights suddenly go out and Eve appears behind us, saving me from the awkward situation.

'Alright, guys. I've locked up the back, let's get out of here.' She attempts to raise a smile, but it doesn't quite reach her eyes.

'What about the dated flowers?' Dawn asks, pointing to the many buckets of discounted stock.

'Just leave them.' Eve mumbles, squeezing past the display. 'We can sort them in the morning.'

I can feel Dawn's eyes burning into the back of my neck and choose to ignore it. Eve never leaves the ruined stock out at the end of the day, *never*. Not wanting to question her, I dump the takings into the safe and grab my coat. Following Eve to the door, I say a silent prayer that the frosty atmosphere between us is all in my imagination. We step outside and stand in silence as Eve proceeds to roll down the heavy shutter. The usual suspects are trundling along the pavement, phones clutched to ears and briefcases banging together in their fight to be the first person to cross the road. Isn't it funny that no matter what life throws at you, people carry on living their lives regardless? When the Lakes rolled out of bed this morning, they firmly believed that their prayers had been answered. They awoke filled with hope that today would be the day that their luck finally changed. I sneak a peek at Eve, who is staring into space with a forlorn look on her face. Her world has come crashing down around her and yet people have still gone to work today, the sun is still high in the sky and the birds are still chirping.

As I am willing myself not to cry, my eyes land on the crazy lady across the street, who is coincidentally packing up for the night, too. Her wiry hair billows in the breeze as she pushes her trolley along the busy street. As usual, the suits dodge her like the plague as she makes her way to the crossing. The numerous plastic bags tied to the trolley rustle loudly, causing her to get more unpleasant looks than usual. Pulling her gaudy cardigan around her body, she shouts at a particular businessman who has clearly rubbed her up the wrong way.

Tearing my eyes away from the comical scene across the street, I zip up my jacket and turn to face the others.

'I'd better shoot.' Dawn covers her mouth as she lets out a yawn. 'Hugh's taking me out for dinner with his parents.'

'His parents?' I squeal, grabbing hold of her arm. 'Eve, did you hear that? Dawn's going to meet the parents!'

Eve looks up at me and rubs her temples. 'I'm sorry, what was that?'

Dawn purses her lips and I feel bad for being giddy when Eve is clearly feeling terrible.

'Nothing.' I shake my head and hold out my hand for hers. 'Come on, let's get home.'

'Actually, I'm going to stick around...'

'You are?' I glance at Dawn and suddenly feel a little concerned.

The fact that Eve lives in the apartment below ours means that we always head home together.

'I'm going to have a look around the shops and maybe get a bite to eat.' She tries to look upbeat, but she isn't fooling anyone.

'Alone? Do you want me to stay with you?' I ask, digging out my phone to tell Oliver that I'll be home late.

'No. I just want to be alone for a little while. I'll see you guys in the morning.'

With a quick wave, Eve secures her shoelaces before running off in the opposite direction. Not quite knowing what to say, I look at Dawn for help.

'You better start talking, because now I'm really worried.' She chews on the tip of her nail and I bat her fingers away.

'It's not my place to say.' I rub my face with both hands, not caring that I am no doubt smearing mascara down my cheeks. 'All you need to know is that Eve asked me for something and I thought I could give it to her, but then I realised I couldn't and now I feel so bad and things are...'

'What the hell are you talking about?' Dawn cuts me off mid-sentence, looking at me as though I have completely lost my mind.

'Just trust me that we aren't ill and we are still friends... I hope.' I give Dawn a hug and shoo her towards the train station. 'Now go. Enjoy your evening and remember, you only get one chance to make a good first impression.'

Heading off towards my apartment, I bury my hands in my pockets and try to block out the world around me. I couldn't feel any worse about the Eve situation if I tried and now all I want is to get home to my two boys. Picking up my pace, I manage to make it back to the apartment in no time at all and practically throw myself into the lift. Spotting Owen's distinct Maserati pull into the car park, I quickly jab at the button and breathe a sigh of relief as the door swings shut. The last thing I want is to be stuck in a lift with Owen for the agonising minute that it takes to reach our floor.

At least Oliver will be happy with my decision, I think to myself as I watch the numbers increase on the screen overhead. I take comfort in that idea as I walk along the hallway to our apartment and slide my key in the door. The first thing I notice is that there's no wagging tail to greet me, the second is that the apartment is eerily quiet. Tossing my keys onto the kitchen island, I pad into the living room and scan the area for my family.

'Hello?' I shout, pushing open our bedroom door and realising that it's empty. 'Is anyone home?'

Hearing a rustling coming from the spare room, I make my way over and reach out for the handle.

'But why?' Noah's little voice cries, stopping me in my tracks. 'It's not fair.'

Pressing my ear against the frame, my heart pounds as I hear Oliver clear his throat.

'I know, son. I wish things were different, too.'

'I'll be OK, Noah.' Janie's voice wavers as she speaks, causing Noah to cry even more. 'Gee-Gee will still come and see you all the time.'

'Come on, don't cry.' Oliver tries to soothe Noah and I wince as a floorboard squeaks beneath my feet.

'Why does Mummy want Gee-Gee to leave?' Noah presses, causing my heart to pound in my chest.

'Well, sometimes grown-ups don't always get along so well. Take MJ for instance. You're friends, right? But you wouldn't want him to live here with us, would you?'

'Yes, I would!' Noah wails, kicking his feet in a tantrum.

'OK, well how about Madison?'

There's a silence and I can just picture Noah shaking his head. Madison and Noah can't play together for more than five minutes without Noah screaming that Madison isn't playing fairly.

'You see? Sometimes you can be buddies with someone, but you don't want to see them all the time. Do you see where I am coming from with this?'

Not being able to listen to another word, I grab my keys and run to the door. Sprinting past the lift, I take the stairs and gallop as fast as my legs will carry me. A couple dive out of the way and exchange quizzical looks as I fire past them and out into the car park. My ears are ringing and I actually feel quite sick. How have things gone so fundamentally wrong in just forty-eight short hours? Picking up my pace, I chew the inside of my cheek to stop myself from crying. It was just thirty minutes ago that I was last here, but the difference in the street is remarkable. Gone are the bustling crowds, gone are the flustered street sellers and gone is the stressful white noise of carrier bags crinkling that fills any hope of silence.

Shoving my hands into my pockets, I take a right and find myself back at Floral Fizz. The wind rustles through my hair as I look up at the sign and wonder if Eve is still around. My entire body aches as I tear my eyes away from the sign. Glancing to my left to check for traffic, I cross the street and slump down on the bench opposite. I feel my phone vibrate in my pocket and deliberately ignore it. I don't want to talk to anyone right now, anyone at all. Pulling my sleeves over my hands, I tip back my head and close my eyes. The evening breeze washes over my face as I inhale deeply, silently praying that it blows away all of my problems.

Just as I am starting to relax, a strange clanging catches my attention. Straining my neck, I look behind me to see the crazy bohemian lady heading my way. It takes me a moment to register that I am sitting in her exact spot. Fighting against the wind, she props her shopping trolley next to the bench and sits down beside me. A strong waft of perfume drifts my way and I can't help but feel pleasantly surprised. I don't quite know why, but I always imagined her to smell like lavender and perhaps stale cigar smoke, but the distinct aroma of Flowerbomb that is dancing around my nostrils is undeniable.

My phone vibrates for a second time and I begrudgingly take it out of my pocket. Seeing Oliver's name pop up on the screen, I jab at the *off* button and place it face down on the bench.

'Life's too short...' My neighbouring friend mumbles, leaning towards me.

'Excuse me?' I reply, completely taken aback by the incredibly posh voice that is coming out of her mouth.

'I said, *life* is far too short.' She runs her fingers through her frazzled hair and I can't help but notice that her hands are dripping in gold rings. 'I've seen that face so many times and let me tell you for a third time, life is too damn short.' I open my mouth to speak, but she continues to talk. 'What is it? A boy?'

Recalling the conversation I just overheard at home, I offer her a small nod and look down at my feet. 'If you must know, it's a boy, a girl, a son and a mother-in-law...'

'Well, that's almost comical, isn't it?' She lets out a laugh and reaches into her tatty old handbag. 'Mint Imperial?'

I look at the torn bag dubiously and shake my head. 'No, thank you.'

Shrugging her shoulders, she pops a couple into her mouth and tosses her handbag back into the trolley with a clang. 'Let's start with the last one. I've always liked to do things back to front. What's the deal with the mother-in-law?'

I roll my neck and try to think of a way to describe Janie that won't result in me screaming out loud or punching a wall.

'Well, she's a handful, put it that way.'

Shaking her head, my new friend reaches into one of her many plastic carrier bags and grabs a box of seeds. 'Just being a handful doesn't result in a face like that...'

I manage a small smile and shield my head as a dozen pigeons flock to our feet. 'It's a long story, but I agreed to have her come and stay with us whilst she got over a divorce, but that was over six months ago and she is driving me insane...'

I take a deep breath and instantly feel a little better for getting things off my chest.

'You know, they do say that a problem shared is a problem halved...' Offering me some bird food, she gives me a smile so kind that it makes me want to cry.

I take a handful of seeds and start to distribute them amongst the pack of pigeons that are waiting greedily.

'You would have to know Janie to understand where I'm coming from. I get that everyone's mother-in-law is a nightmare, but mine really is something else...'

Starting with the first time I met her, I reel off everything that has ever happened between Janie and I. The entire story, right from the beginning. My stomach churns as I recall our disastrous trip to Mexico and despite her efforts to hide it, I notice my new friend grin as I fill her in on Janie's outrageous antics. Once I start, I can't seem to stop and when I eventually pause for breath, she is looking at me with wide eyes.

'Well, that's just *not* OK. You're a young woman. You need to focus on your own marriage before that ends in divorce, too. These are the years that you will look back on and wish that you had lived to the max. Believe me, I know.'

Throwing the last seed and watching the flock of birds fight like crazy over it, I let out a sigh and drop my head. Soon realising that there's no food left, the pigeons abandon us in search of their next victim. Before I can stop myself, I tell her about Oliver's sudden bond with Janie and Noah's heart-wrenching reaction to her being made to leave.

'That's quite a predicament that you've got yourself into there, isn't it?'

'It certainly is...'

Fiddling with the zip on my jacket, I suddenly realise that I don't even know my new friend's name.

'I'm Clara, by the way.' I hold out my hand for hers.

'Sandra.' She stares at me for a moment before accepting my hand.

I give her hand a shake and notice that she has impeccable nails for a homeless person.

'If I could give you one piece of advice from an old woman, it would be to let it go.' Sandra stares at me, her brown eyes suddenly serious.

'Let it go?' I repeat in confusion.

She nods along and shoots a passing businessman a filthy look which I pretend not to notice. 'The number of years that I wasted in my marriage bickering over things that didn't matter is probably one of my biggest regrets.'

'You're married?' I exclaim, probably a little too loudly as a couple of passers-by glance over in our direction.

'Twenty years.' Sandra breathes, holding out her hand to show me her incredible bridal set.

The diamonds shine brightly under the evening sun and I look up at Sandra's face feeling rather confused. Ever since my first day at Floral Fizz, I have watched her sit right here and hurl abuse at the people who walk by. The life I had imagined her living is a million miles away from this middle class, obscenely posh woman with a twenty-year marriage under her belt.

'Sandra, what's your secret?' I ask, taking a closer look at her. 'Twenty years is such a long time...'

'Patience and lots of it.' She fires back, shaking her head as she speaks. 'These days there's only one thing that Ken and I argue about and that's his bloody job.'

'Oh...' I try to picture what kind of man a woman like Sandra would be married to.

'Work, work and more work. That's all he does anymore. I remember the days before he was made partner where we didn't have two pennies to rub together, but we were *happy*. So very happy.' Sandra smiles and looks down at her wedding ring fondly. 'He doesn't remember it like that though. Ken just remembers the struggles, the hard times where we had to scramble around just to put food on the table.' She blows a stray curl out of her face and motions across the street. 'I see these so-called business types marching along, shouting orders into their phones like it's the only thing that matters and I get so angry.'

A light bulb goes off in my mind's eye and I suddenly get an insight into why Sandra spends her days shouting abuse at the suits.

'Ken's married to me, but he's also married to his job and a big part of me hates him for it.' Reaching into her shopping trolley, she pulls out a bouquet of lilies and drops them onto my lap. 'See this? *This* is the most attention that my Ken pays to me. He leaves me home for days on end and when he eventually returns, he has a bunch of damn flowers. Like flowers can compensate for his absence, for my loneliness.'

I turn over the flowers in my hands when a thought suddenly hits me. I know these flowers! I know them because *I'm* the one who wrapped them! Mr Williams! Mr Williams is Sandra's husband! I bite my lip and feel weirdly guilty. Should I tell her that I am the woman who helps to choose the flowers that she so clearly despises?

Licking my lips, I straighten out the tissue paper carefully. 'You know... *I* think a man who buys his wife flowers so frequently can't be all that bad.' Sandra takes the flowers back and gives them a moment's glance before dropping them into the trolley. 'I happen to work in a florist's, and I know a certain gentleman who gushes like crazy about the wife that he loves so dearly...'

She shoots me a sideways glance and squints her eyes. 'You do?'

'I do. I can't tell you how many times he's bent my ear over how he needs the perfect bouquet for his beloved wife. He must have made his way through the entire brochure. Roses, daffodils, tulips and most recently, lilies.'

I purse my lips as Sandra tucks her wiry hair behind her ears, looking deep in thought. I don't need to spell it out for her. She knows exactly who I am talking about. Taking a deep breath, I look up at Floral Fizz just in time to see Eve walking past the shop. Her arms laden with shopping bags, she struggles to balance the many purchases as she makes her way towards the apartment.

'You never told me about the girl?' Sandra muses, putting one hand on the shopping trolley.

I shield my eyes from the evening sun and smile as Eve disappears around the corner. 'On second thoughts, I don't think the girl is much of a problem after all.'

'Well, I'm pleased to hear that you have one less thing to worry about.' Pushing herself to her feet,

Sandra rearranges her selection of carrier bags and holds out her hand. 'It's been a pleasure to meet you, Clara. Now, go back to that lovely family of yours and decide what is *really* important.'

I look down at my wedding set and nod in response. Watching her walk away, shouting random curse words at a couple of power-dressed women, I rest my chin in my hand and try to gather my thoughts. Do I want my marriage to end up like Sandra's? When I said my vows, I promised to love Oliver through sickness and through health. Well, I think it's safe to say that Janie is his sickness. Standing up, I walk as slowly as possible across the deserted street.

The sun shines in my eyes as I look back for Sandra. Not being able to spot her, I start to make my way back home. Isn't it strange how you can be so terribly wrong about a person? Meeting Sandra has opened my eyes. She has made me realise that you shouldn't judge the journey until you have walked the path, because who knows, you might have fallen at the very first step…

Chapter 13

Staring at the apartment door, I try to steady my breathing before sliding my key into the lock and stepping inside. Pumpkin dashes over from her place in front of the television and jumps up at me excitedly. The absence of her collar tells me that she's been out for her daily walk with Summer. Crouching down to the floor, I run my fingers through her fluffy coat and smile as she rolls onto her back. Her tail wags furiously as I reach up to the treat cupboard and swap a dog biscuit for a wet kiss on the nose. Tearing myself away from my furbaby, I slip my keys into my pocket and knock lightly on Janie's door.

'Come in.' Janie's Texan drawl hollers, above the banging that is going on inside.

Popping my head around the door, my jaw drops open as I take in the scene in front of me. Gone are the mouldy plates, the piles of dirty laundry and the mountain of empty Xanax packets. The bedding has been freshly laundered, the carpets have been vacuumed and most obviously, Janie's cases appear to be packed.

'I've been trying to call you.' Oliver mumbles, from his place at the foot of the bed.

'Yeah, we tried to call your phone!' Noah runs towards me and jumps into my arms. 'Where were you?'

'I was at work.' I whisper, burying my face into his warm neck.

'Until this time?' Oliver glances at his watch and frowns.

'I went for a walk. I needed to, you know, *think* about things...' I look over at Janie who is standing by her suitcase with an abandoned look on her face. 'It looks like you guys have been busy.'

'We have!' Noah squeals excitedly. 'We cleaned up Gee-Gee's room!'

'I can see that.' I gush, widening my eyes to emphasise my joy at the clean room. 'Noah, why don't you go and make a start on your room whilst I talk to your dad and Gee-Gee?'

Noah pauses for a moment before jumping down. 'OK, but only if I can watch television before bed.'

'Deal.' I say, holding out my hand to seal the deal.

Watching Noah grab Pumpkin and run out of the room, I gently shut the door and walk over to the bed. 'Can we talk, please?'

I'm half expecting Janie to kick off and tell me that we said everything that we needed to say last night, but to my surprise, she motions for me to sit down. My lips become incredibly dry as I try to figure out what exactly it is that I want to say. After a long pause, I look up at Janie and sigh heavily.

'You don't have to go, Janie.' Oliver holds his breath and I try not to look at him. 'You drive me insane. You make me think that I'm actually losing my mind, but just because I don't *like* you all the time, doesn't mean that I don't *love* you.'

I hear Oliver let out a gasp and I can't say that I blame him. It's true that I can't stand to live with Janie and it's also true that I despise her behaviour, but I don't hate her, not really, anyway.

'I pushed the boundaries.' Janie's bottom lip wobbles as she sits down beside me. 'I knew I was doing it, but something inside me just snapped.' She pauses for a moment and composes herself. 'I was with Randy since I was just a girl. I guess I never got the chance to let my hair down. For the first time in my life, I had the opportunity to have no responsibilities and be I dunno, *free.*'

We lock eyes and for the first time, I can see the person behind the bravado. 'I can understand that.'

I lean over to wipe a tear from her cheek, but almost as quickly as the mask slipped, it is firmly back in place.

'Oliver and I have been talking and it's time for me to move on.' I open my mouth to protest, but Oliver silences me with a shake of the head. 'I've been avoiding my life back in Texas for long enough now. I have to face the music. It's time for me to go home.'

Turning around to face Oliver, he nods and reaches out for my hand. 'We had a long talk and Mom's right, it's time for her to go back to America.'

'Are you sure that's what you want?' I ask, looking between the two of them anxiously.

They nod simultaneously as Noah comes tearing into the room, quickly followed by Pumpkin.

'I've cleaned it!' He announces, falling to the floor and feigning exhaustion. 'Pumpkin helped.'

The three of us watch Noah and Pumpkin rolling around on the carpet for a while, enjoying the comfortable silence. I suddenly remember Noah's wish and feel a wave of sadness.

'Hey, Noah, come up here a second.' I pat my knee and let out a groan as he throws himself into my arms. 'Your dad and I wanted to talk to you for a minute.'

'Am I in trouble?' He asks, looking up at Oliver mournfully.

'Not at all.' Oliver shakes his head and crouches down to Noah's level. 'Gee-Gee is going to go back to Texas.'

'No!' Noah's face falls and he shakes his head. 'What about my wish?'

'Wish?' Oliver's brow creases into a frown. 'What wish?'

'Noah and I had a race yesterday and he won a wish.' Clearing my throat, my cheeks colour up as I speak. 'He wished that his Gee-Gee didn't have to go...'

Janie lets out a squawk and rubs Noah's shoulder. 'I don't *have* to go, Noah, but I want to.'

'You do?' He rubs his eyes and I feel my heart break yet again.

Janie nods and purses her lips. 'I do, but I'm going to come back and see you all the time, you hear me?'

Sensing that Janie is on the verge of tears, I blink away my own and jump off the bed.

'Alright, who's ready for some dinner?' I hold my own hand in the air and giggle as Noah stands to attention.

'I am!'

'I think we all are.' Oliver yawns and leans over to squeeze his mother's hand.

'What do you say, Janie? Can you face one final meal of saturated fats and complex carbohydrates?'

She turns around and checks out her backside in the mirror. 'I think my ass can handle one more. Yours? Not so much...'

Not knowing whether to laugh or cry, I stare at Janie in shock.

'I'm kidding!' She roars, throwing back her head and cackling like a rabid hyena. 'Let's get outta here…'

* * *

Looking up at the ceiling, I inhale deeply and feel the stress practically drift away from my body. Tonight has been the best night we have had since Janie arrived. Rather than cooking, the four of us grabbed our coats and went to McDonald's. You heard me. We actually managed to get *Janie* into a *McDonald's* and what's more shocking is that she didn't complain once. We did consider something fancier, but with her booking her flights to Texas before we left, an all-American farewell seemed fitting. I hate to admit it, but she really does seem to have had a personality transplant. Well, apart from the odd dig about my decision to order large fries and flirting with the adolescent server, but I guess Janie will always be Janie deep down.

Picturing her tickle Noah until he cried happy tears, I almost feel bad for being the instigator in making her leave, but whilst Janie used the little girl's room, Oliver actually thanked me for making him tackle this head on. It seems that he had been burying his head in the sand for a while now and despite his initial protest, he didn't know how to handle the situation for the best. Looking back on the series of events that has led us to where we are today, I can completely understand why. I mean, what choice did he have? He couldn't exactly tell her to leave when she was clearly in the middle of some kind of post-divorce breakdown.

Flicking off the bathroom light, Oliver strips off his t-shirt and crawls into bed next to me. He lets out a lion worthy yawn and flops back onto the pillows.

'Thank you.' He whispers, wrapping his arms around my waist and squeezing me tightly.

'What for?' I roll over to face him and run my fingers through his hair.

'For everything.' He brings his eyes up to meet mine and my stomach flips like crazy. 'For putting up with my mom all this time. For not packing up and leaving yourself. For not pressuring me to make her leave.'

'I don't think I can take credit for that last one...' Blood rushes to my cheeks and I tear my eyes away from his.

'Are you kidding me? Most women would have kicked my ass *months* ago with the way my mom has been acting.' He rolls onto his back and shoves another pillow behind his head. 'I'm genuinely sorry that I didn't back you up on her behaviour. The mess, the cursing, the goddam men...' He screws up his nose and exhales sharply. 'I just felt torn. I felt like I was stuck in the middle of my mom and my wife. I knew she was in the wrong, of course I did...'

'You don't need to explain yourself.' Planting a soft kiss on his cheek, I curl up on his chest and allow my eyes to close. 'I understand.'

'Well, I just want you to know that I'm very aware of what an amazing wife I have...'

A smile plays on my lips as my eyelids become suddenly heavy. Before I can stop it, my mind flits to the Lakes and my stomach does a flip. 'I don't think Owen and Eve think I'm very amazing right now...'

'What do you mean?' Oliver mumbles, as he starts to fall asleep.

'I told them I couldn't do it.' My skin prickles as I recall the coffee shop disaster. 'It was awful. Honestly, it was absolutely awful. I felt terrible.'

Oliver runs his fingers along my spine and sighs. 'I can't imagine how difficult that was for you, but if it's any consolation, I think you made the right decision.'

I attempt to smile, but the guilt that is in my heart is hard to ignore. I know that he's right, but it doesn't stop me from feeling incredibly bad about it.

'It will happen for them, but this wasn't the answer.' He pulls me closer and I shuffle over to make room for Pumpkin, who has dived onto the foot of the bed with her favourite toy. I look down at her adorable face as she settles down to go to sleep.

'I feel like Pumpkin is going to end up my only friend at this rate...'

'Don't be ridiculous!' Oliver laughs and plants a kiss on my forehead. 'Speaking of friends, Li called while you were out.'

'What did she say?' I gasp, flipping over to face him.

With everything that has been going on, I had totally forgotten about Lianna's visit!

'Well, you will be pleased to know that they land tomorrow afternoon.' He pauses whilst I let out a squeal. 'Apparently, she's going to meet you at Eve's book club. I did question why she would want to go to a *book club* after a long-haul flight, but she seemed pretty set on it.'

I hide a grin behind my frizzy curls and nod in response. Lianna's insistence on coming to our book club doesn't surprise me in the slightest. Not wanting to give the game away on our Friday night cocktail sessions, I kiss him goodnight and close my eyes. Janie's heading back to America, Oliver and I have reconnected, the Lakes will forgive me... *eventually* and my best friend is coming home. It seems that the storm has finally passed...

Chapter 14

When I peel my eyes open the following morning, I promise myself that today is going to be a good day. Stretching out my legs, I roll out of bed and practically dance into the bathroom. The sun streams in through the window as I grab my dressing gown from the back of the door. Standing on the tips of my toes, I push open the window and fill my lungs with crisp fresh air. Since Oliver left earlier, I have tossed, turned and literally counted down the minutes until it was an acceptable time to get up.

I must have called Lianna a million times already. I've also tried texting, emailing, Skyping and every other social media account I can think of, but nothing has proved effective. I know, I am very aware that I will be seeing her in the flesh in just a few short hours, but I have never had any patience, especially when it comes to Li. Our friendship has been tested so much since she left and I am absolutely ecstatic that she is coming home. They say that true friendship lasts the length of time. Well, ours has lasted time, distance, break-ups and meltdowns. Carlsberg don't make friendships, but if they did, they would have made ours.

Flicking off the bathroom light, I stroll across the bedroom and throw open the door to the living room. To my surprise, Noah is already up and even more surprisingly, so is Janie.

'Good morning!' She hollers, from her place at the kitchen island.

I widen my eyes in shock and make my way over to where she and Noah are sitting. 'Good morning to you guys, too. What are we eating over here?'

'Pancakes!' Noah yells, holding up his plate with sticky fingers. 'Do you want some?'

'Umm...' I eye up the pool of chocolate sauce dubiously.

'No, she doesn't.' Janie mumbles, taking a sip from her coffee mug and pointing to the oven. 'I've done your mom bacon and eggs.' She flashes me a wink and piles more pancakes onto Noah's plate. 'Eggs over easy, just as you like them.'

My stomach rumbles greedily as I squeeze by her and take a steaming plate out of the oven.

'What's all this in aid of?' I ask, grabbing the brown sauce and completely covering my bacon. 'You *never* cook!'

'I cook!' She protests, popping a grape into her mouth and frowning.

'Please!' I try to laugh, but having a mouthful of delicious bacon prevents me from doing so. 'Pouring shop-bought hummus into a bowl, does *not* count as cooking.'

'She made my pancakes!' Noah points out, shoving the last piece into his mouth.

'She did?' I jab my fork into a piece of toast and groan as it slips straight onto the floor. 'Dammit...'

I pause for a moment, waiting for Pumpkin to sweep in and hoover it up. 'Where's Pumpkin?' I ask, when her familiar snout doesn't appear under the table.

Janie points over her shoulder to the balcony and I let out a giggle as I see her tearing back and forth along the balcony. Bless her. If everyone was as happy as Pumpkin, the world would be a much better place. Dragging my eyes away from her fluffy butt, I pick up the offending toast and make a second attempt at tackling my breakfast.

'I hear Lianna's back today.' Janie muses, raising her eyebrows a millimetre as she nurses her mug.

I nod in response and head over to the coffee machine. 'I know! I can't tell you how excited I am to see her!'

'I'm more excited to meet the mysterious Vernon...' Her eyes glint wickedly as she smacks her lips together. 'I hear he's quite the dish...'

'What's a dish?' Noah asks, his little brow creasing into a confused frown as he reaches for his glass of water.

I lock eyes with Janie and shake my head.

'Never you mind. Now eat your breakfast...'

* * *

'Can we race again?' Noah begs, slamming the door shut behind us. 'Please? Please? Please?'

I roll my eyes and adjust the strap on my shoe. 'Go on then, but no cheating!'

'I don't cheat!' He exclaims, clearly offended at being labelled a trickster.

'Mmm...' I hold on to the bannister and stick out my tongue. 'On the count of three?' Noah positions himself like Usain Bolt and nods. 'One... two... *three!*'

The pair of us set off and even though I try to win this time, Noah soars on ahead of me. Unsurprisingly, he reaches the top before I even hit the second flight of steps and fist-pumps the air.

'I'm just too quick for you, aren't I, Mummy?'

I let out a laugh and hope that breaking a sweat hasn't ruined my make-up. 'Yes, I think you are.'

Holding out my hand for his, I let him drag me towards Gina's apartment. Suddenly stopping in his tracks, Noah drops his backpack onto the floor and tugs on my sleeve.

'Mummy, because I won the race, do I get another wish?' He looks up at me and crosses his fingers behind his back. 'Because my last one didn't come true...'

My heart breaks for him, but I do my best to hide my feelings behind a strained grin. 'Well, I guess you *did* win the race, but you better make it quick. Gina will be waiting for you.'

'That's OK, because I already know what I want.' He shoots me his cutest smile and bats his ridiculously long eyelashes. 'I want another puppy.'

I stare at him for a moment, feeling completely flummoxed. There's more chance of Janie staying than Oliver agreeing to have another dog in the apartment.

'Well...' I try to think of something to say that won't make me break yet another promise to my son.

'Or I could wish for a bike?' He beams up at me cheekily and raises his eyebrows. 'Deal?'

'You are most definitely your father's son.' A laugh escapes my lips as he grabs the hem of my coat and drags me towards Gina's apartment. 'Deal.'

Rapping on the door, I hold Noah's lunchbox under my arm and pretend to listen as Noah tells me exactly which bike he wants. After standing there for a good minute, I exchange confused glances with Noah and give it another knock. Eventually the door swings open, but it's not Gina who's standing there, it's Eve.

'Oh...' I offer her a surprised smile and step inside. 'What are you doing here?'

'I just needed to speak to Gina.' Eve leans down and ruffles Noah's hair. 'How's it going, Noah?'

'I'm getting a bike!' He exclaims, throwing his arms in the air and rushing past her.

'Wasn't it Noah's birthday *last* month?' Eve asks, clearly concerned that she has missed his birthday.

'It was, but this isn't a birthday gift.' I drop his lunchbox by the door and fold my arms. 'He had a wish.' Eve looks at me puzzled as Gina appears behind her. 'It's a long story...'

'Hey!' Gina smiles broadly and hitches up her leggings. 'How are you? Feeling better today?'

It takes me a minute to recall what she's talking about. 'Yes, I am feeling much better now. Thanks for asking.'

'You sure?' Gina scrunches up her nose and picks up Melrose, who is jumping up and down at her feet. 'You seemed pretty upset yesterday.'

Eve looks between the two of us and I shoot Gina a *please shut up* glare. 'I'm fine, honestly.'

Clearly getting the hint, Gina purses her lips and tries to stop Melrose from pulling out her earrings.

'Anyway, we should probably get going.' Eve checks the time on her mobile and beckons for me to follow her. 'We shall see you tonight though!'

'Definitely!' Gina cackles, taking Noah's lunchbox and throwing it over her shoulder. 'I believe we are having another member this evening?'

My stomach flutters as she chats animatedly with Eve about Lianna's impending arrival. Just a few hours to go! Well, nine to be precise, but who's counting? Saying our goodbyes, we make our way along the lobby to the stairs.

'So, how was the shopping?' I ask, giving Eve's arm a little nudge.

She gives me a confused look and continues down the staircase. 'I'm sorry?'

'Yesterday? When we left work, you said you were going shopping?' I squint my eyes as I try to work out what's going on with her.

'Oh, yes. I kind of went a little crazy, but you're allowed to do a little retail therapy when you feel down, aren't you?' She lets out a nervous laugh and marches on ahead.

My blood runs cold as I stare at the back of my friend and I know that we can't ignore the elephant in the room for any longer. Eve and I have built up such an open and honest friendship over the years, I will be damned if I am going to lose her. Stopping midway down the second flight of stairs, I drop my handbag to the floor with a thud and take a seat on the nearest step.

'What are you doing?' Eve asks, obviously perplexed as to why I am sitting down in the middle of the public stairway.

I tap the space beside me and hold out my hand for hers. 'We need to talk...'

Hesitating for a second, she gingerly scans the area before sitting down, taking extra care not to let anything touch her beloved handbag.

'I'm sorry, Eve. I really, really am.' My bottom lip starts to tremble, and I inwardly scold myself for losing my composure so soon. 'I don't want to lose you as a friend...'

'What?' Eve exclaims, her jaw dropping open. 'Why on earth would you lose me? I've been worried sick that *I* am going to lose *you*!' She looks up at the ceiling and blinks rapidly. 'I should never have put you in that position, Clara. I just, I don't know, I was desperate. I *am* desperate.'

A tear slips down my cheek and I wipe it away before she can see. 'I am flattered, *honoured* even that you asked me. I just wish I...'

'You don't need to explain yourself. I completely understand.' Eve shakes her head and squeezes my hand tightly. 'Egg donation isn't how this is going to happen for us, but it *is* going to happen. I know it.'

I rub her shoulder encouragingly and smile. 'That's more like it. Think positive. Think like the Eve that we all know and love. You can *make* this happen. I know you can. You just need to find the right path to lead you there...'

'You're right.' She sniffs loudly and wipes the mascara rings from beneath her eyes. 'And in the meantime, we have been at it like rabbits! I mean, it can't hurt, can it?'

I let out a gasp as Mrs Milton from apartment 304 strides past and shoots us a filthy look.

'You couldn't have timed that any better if you tried!' I whisper, feeling like a naughty schoolgirl.

Visibly appalled at the idea of a married couple having sex, Mrs Milton curses under her breath as she flees down the staircase. Waiting until she has left the building, Eve rests her head on my shoulder as we burst into a fit of giggles.

'Come on. Let's go to work...'

* * *

'What do you think?' Dawn bites her nail furiously as she stares at me with hungry eyes. 'Well, say something!'

'I... I don't really know what I think.' I look over at Eve who is staring at Dawn with glassy eyes. 'Eve, what do *you* think?'

'I think it's amazing.' She gushes, leaning across the counter and smiling erratically.

'Eve!' I hiss, panic rising in my throat. 'Don't encourage her!'

A loved-up grin spreads across Dawn's face and I wag my finger at her like a teacher. 'Just think about it for a moment. Like *actually* think about it.'

I hold my breath as Dawn folds her arms and looks deep in thought. The shop is so quiet that you can hear the clock ticking on the wall. Realising that she is taking her time over this, I distract myself by arranging the roses until I can't take it a second longer.

'Well, say something!' I exclaim, throwing my hands in the air.

'I've thought about it and I am going to do it.' She clutches her hands to her face and squeals. 'I'm going to marry Hugh!'

'This is amazing!' Eve squeals like a child at Christmas and jumps up and down the spot. 'Congratulations! We have *so* much planning to do...'

I chew the inside of my cheek as I watch the two of them embracing. Dawn's getting married. She's getting married to a man that she met exactly seven days ago today. The man who only a few days ago I had to literally *force* her to go out for lunch with.

'I know what you're thinking.' Dawn gasps for breath and hastily rearranges her hair. 'You're thinking that I've only known him for a week and on Wednesday I was a little *hesitant* to meet him for lunch.' I brush my curls out of my face and shrug my shoulders. 'I know what you're thinking, because *I'm* thinking it too! It's crazy. It's insane. It's...' Looking around to ensure that the shop is free from customers, Dawn leans over the counter so that she is just inches from my face. 'Do you remember why I took this job?' She whispers, so quietly that I can hardly hear her.

I tilt my head to one side as I recall the story that Dawn told me many times before. 'The fortune teller?'

She nods in response and bites her lip. 'Well, when she told me that I would stumble into this job, she also told me that it would lead me to my future husband!'

My eyes widen as I try to work if she's is joking. 'You can't be serious?'

'I'm *totally* serious!' Dawn giggles like a love-struck teenager. 'She promised that my new career would be where I would meet him and get this, she told me he would be called Harry!'

'But Hugh isn't called Harry. He's called *Hugh*...' I look at her as though she has lost her mind and frown.

'It's close enough!' Dawn laughs and punches my arm playfully. 'Think of it this way, the fortune teller was so right about this job being the best decision I would ever make. Taking her advice has led me to a job where I can't wait to get out of bed in the morning. It has led me to making the best friends that a girl could ask for and now it has led me to the man I am going to marry.' She inhales deeply and looks between

Eve and I. 'She was so right about the job, just imagine if she was right about this too...'

Eve reaches for the tissues and I have to admit that I could do with one as well. 'Well, when you put it like that...'

Dawn and Eve shriek simultaneously and I can't help but join in. 'I still think it's crazy, but you're crazy and I wish you all the happiness in the world.'

We have a group bear hug and I can't help but feel happy for Dawn. Yes, seven days is a ridiculously short amount of time to know someone before agreeing to spend the rest of your life with them, but Lianna did pretty much the same thing with Vernon and look how happy she is now. Thinking of Lianna makes my skin tingle with anticipation. Stealing a glance at my watch, I am about to ask Eve if I can sneak outside to call her when the doorbell chimes loudly. Jumping apart, we snap back into work mode and stand to attention.

'Mr Williams!' I exclaim, placing my hands face down on the counter. 'I didn't expect to see you again so soon.' Eve and Dawn scuttle into the back of the shop to arrange the afternoon delivery, so I grab my apron and motion to the brochure. 'What can I get for you today?'

Mr Williams beams widely and adjusts the waistband on his jeans. I don't think I've ever seen him out of his office clothes before. 'Actually, today *I* won't be the one choosing.'

I flash him a quizzical look which melts into a smile as Sandra walks into the florist's. Looking as crazy as ever, she strides across the floor in an orange kaftan and takes Ken's hand in hers.

'We won't be needing that brochure.' Sandra looks at me and winks. 'I know *exactly* what I would like.' I try to keep a straight look on my face and play dumb as she dumps her handbag on the counter.

'And what would that be?'

'Sunflowers.' She declares proudly. 'Your biggest, most vibrant bunch of sunflowers.'

'Sunflowers?' I repeat, very aware that of the dozens of bouquets I have made up for Mr Williams, sunflowers are probably the one and only flower that I haven't used.

Clearly realising this too, Ken shifts his weight from one foot to the other. 'You've never said that you like sunflowers.' He mumbles, wiping a bead of sweat from his forehead.

Sandra exhales and blows her frizzy fringe out of her eyes. 'You never asked...'

I hold my breath as they look at each other carefully, the love between the two of them filling the room.

'Clara, we shall take a bouquet of your finest sunflowers and can you set up a standing order so that my beautiful wife can have her favourite flowers every week of the year?' Ken slams his credit card onto the counter with a flourish, causing Sandra to grin brightly.

Feeling a little overwhelmed, I give him a swift nod and make a grab for the roll of tissue paper. As I pluck several striking sunflowers and position them between the sheets of paper, Mr Williams and Sandra watch me in complete silence. I am smiling at my frankly beautiful creation when Sandra reaches over and taps my arm.

'There's a smile that speaks a thousand words...'

I contemplate thanking her for making me see things more clearly, but the way that she is beaming at me tells me that she already knows.

We lock eyes as I hand over the bouquet of flowers. 'There you are, Mrs Williams. You are one lucky lady.'

Sandra glances over at Mr Williams, who is now beaming from ear to ear.

'I most certainly am...'

Chapter 15

Music floods into the toilet cubicle as I struggle to fasten the zipper on my skinny jeans. Why do I never learn? Skin-tight denim is *not* the ideal attire when you plan on drinking your weight in bubbles all night. Juggling my clutch bag and mobile phone, I slide open the lock and check out my reflection in the mirror. Eyeliner is still in place and the lip gloss I blindly applied earlier hasn't made its way onto my teeth, not bad considering that I've sunk almost an entire bottle of fizz. Taking my bronzer out of my bag, I apply yet another layer to my cheeks. Lianna's been living in *Barbados*, I'm not being plastered all over Facebook looking like Casper the ghost if I can help it.

Checking my phone for what feels like the millionth time, I place my hands under the running water before slipping back into the bar. As usual, Artemis is buzzing with people, all alive with that delicious Friday feeling. We have been here for just over an hour and I still haven't been able to get in touch with Li and even though Vernon called Oliver when they got off the plane, a small part of me is worried that they aren't really coming. I flash Eve a grin as I slide back into my seat, pricking my ears to pick up on the conversation. Unsurprisingly, the topic on everyone's lips has become Dawn's sudden decision to marry a near stranger.

'I say go for it!' Gina cackles, waving her glass around in the air. 'You get *one* life and before you know it you have three babies, a laundry basket that's never empty and an impending fortieth birthday.'

Janie nods along and clinks her glass against Gina's. 'Besides, you can always just divorce him if it doesn't work out.'

I shake my head in response to Janie's crude remark and dump my handbag on the table. When I filled the girls in on my huge turnaround with Janie and her decision to return to America, they all insisted that I invite her along tonight. Looking at her now, laughing and joking with the girls, I have to admit that I am glad I did. Fiddling with the strap of my watch, I am cursing myself for drinking so much in such a short space of time when a distant rumbling catches my attention.

'Is that thunder?' I whisper to Gina, looking out of the window expecting to see a storm coming in.

'I don't think so, but I did hear something.' Straining her neck, she scans the room before letting out a scream and slamming down her glass.

The rest of us fall into silence as we watch her sprint across the room.

'What's she doing?' Dawn picks up the cocktail menu and flips through the pages, more interested in choosing her next tipple.

Standing on the tips of my toes, my heart pounds in my chest as a familiar face enters the bar.

'Is that...' Eve's voice trails off as I let out a shriek of my own.

'Vernon!' I squeal, clapping my hands together excitedly and running over.

Already embracing Gina, Vernon reaches out and scoops me up with his free hand.

'Hey!' He lets out a low laugh and squeezes the two of us tightly. 'How's it going?'

'I'm great!' I plant a kiss on his cheek and look behind him for Lianna. 'Where is she?'

'She's right there!' He points over to the bar and allows Gina to drag him to the pack of waiting girls.

Squeezing through the gathering of people, I tap the shoulder of an insanely brown and pink-haired Lianna.

'Li?' I let out a gasp as she spins around and throws her long arms around my neck.

Clinging on to her for fear that she will disappear, I bury my face in her hair and breathe in her familiar perfume. She's here! She's actually here! Not wanting to let go, we stand there for a good few minutes before finally tearing ourselves apart.

'You look amazing!' I gush, running my fingers through her striking new haircut.

'So do you!' Lianna looks me up and down and nods approvingly. 'I *love* those shoes!'

'You do?' I hold them up for her to see the gems more clearly. 'I got them in the sales!'

As I lead Lianna over to our table, I fill her in on last month's epic shopping session. Isn't it incredible that no matter how much time we spend apart, the second we're together again it's like she never left? Before I can say another word, Eve fires out of her seat and leaps up at Li. My heart bursts with pride as I step back and watch my friends greet each other animatedly. They say that friends are the family we choose for ourselves and if that is the case, I have chosen the best family a girl could wish for.

Not wanting to interrupt, I sip my drink and watch as Eve introduces Dawn to Lianna and Janie to

Vernon. Just as I expected, Janie's jaw drops open as she eyes up Vernon like he is a hot pecan pie. As much as I hate to admit it, I am going to miss that woman, just don't tell her, ever.

Once we are all sitting down, I motion to the barman to bring over more fizz and a couple of glasses for the new arrivals.

'So, how was the flight?' I ask, not being able to stop myself from smiling happily.

'Long!' They answer in unison, accepting a glass each and clinking them together.

Lianna takes a sip of the crisp bubbles and swoons. I am about to ask her if she upgraded her seats when she picks up a fork from the table and taps her glass.

'Alright, before we move on to other things, Vernon and I have a couple of things to tell you all...'

The rest of us exchange concerned glances as my heart pounds in my chest. 'All good, I hope?'

'Very good.' Vernon confirms, kicking back in his seat and stretching out his long legs.

'First things first...' Li tucks her hair behind her ears and puts down her glass. 'I have gifts!'

A chorus of oohs echoes around the room as Lianna reaches into a hot pink holdall. Producing a brown paper bag, she passes around a selection of delicate shell bracelets. Each one has shades of lemon, lilac and mint, all held together with a pretty ivory rope.

'Where's mine?' Eve frowns, tipping the bag upside down to show Lianna that it is empty.

'You've got an *extra special* gift...' Vernon teases, taking a black pouch from his pocket and handing it over. 'This came from my mom. Her instructions were that you use it daily, twice daily for optimum results.'

Eve takes the velvet bag and fiddles with the ribbon, her face alight with anticipation. Pouring out the contents into her lap, she turns over a stunning green stone in her hands.

'What is it?' She asks, holding up the nugget to the light.

'It's jade.' Lianna explains. 'You're supposed to rub it on your stomach to increase fertility. I know you might think it's silly, but I thought it was worth a shot.'

The room falls into silence as we wait with bated breath for Eve's reaction. I know Lianna means well, but I also know that anything baby related is a sore spot with Eve.

'Well, in that case, rub me up good and proper!' She lets out a laugh and passes the stone around the group.

One by one, we take the beautiful gem and rub it vigorously on Eve's tiny tummy. The smooth stone is cold in my hands as I say a silent prayer and press it against her stomach.

'Thank you.' Eve gushes holding on to the green gem as though her life depends on it. 'I'm going to use this every single day until I have a bun in the oven.'

Lianna flashes her the thumbs-up sign and pulls a yellow box from her handbag. 'We also got you this. It's just a pregnancy test. I thought a Bajan one might be luckier for you.'

If you didn't know Lianna, you would probably think this is a little strange, but Li is more superstitious than anyone I've ever met.

Eve laughs and places it on the table next to the jade stone. 'You know what, the next test I take is going to be this one.'

'Talking of tests, when did you last take one?' Gina asks, scooting her chair forwards and turning over the box in her hands.

'A couple of weeks ago with Clara.' Eve looks down into her orange juice and sighs. 'I haven't wanted to take another, to be honest.'

I nod along as I recall Eve's heartbroken face as she looked into that little window.

'You've still been trying though, right?' Gina places the test back on the table.

'Oh, we've been trying alright!' Eve manages a small smile. 'We have been doing it literally every day, ovulating or not!'

Vernon's cheeks flush pink and we fall about laughing.

'Weeks of extreme baby-making and you haven't taken a test?' Janie howls, topping up her glass with the bottle on the table. 'Go get that test done!'

Eve chews her lip and looks around the group dubiously. 'Should I?'

'Yes!' We all yell at once, shooing her towards the toilets.

Taking one last gulp of her drink, Eve grabs the yellow box and stands to her feet.

'Before you go.' Lianna pulls Eve back by her sleeve. 'There's something we wanted to tell you guys.'

Vernon beams brightly as Li looks up at him. 'We have decided to sell The Hangout...'

'What?' I exclaim, cutting him off midsentence. 'Why?'

'It's all happened so quickly.' A smile plays on Lianna's lips as she runs her fingers along the glass. 'We had a call from Prestige, you know, the five-star hotel around the bay?'

Eve, Gina and I nod along, knowing exactly what she is talking about because we have all been there.

'Well, they wanted to buy the bar.' Vernon sighs and drapes his arm around Lianna's shoulders. 'At first, I said *no*, I mean, The Hangout has been my life, but then they upped their offer...'

'And then upped it again!' Li chips in, her face flush with glee.

'To what?' I ask, before I can stop myself.

Lianna giggles and clutches her hands to her face. 'It was at least six figures, put it that way.'

A gasp echoes around our group and my entire body tingles with excitement. They're selling The Hangout! I don't quite believe it!

'So...' She continues, her eyes sparkling. 'This brings us on to our final announcement.' Entwining her fingers with Vernon's, she clears her throat dramatically. 'We have decided... to move back to London!'

I stare at her in disbelief as Gina and Eve throw themselves at the two of them, not quite sure that I have heard her correctly. 'You're moving back?' I manage, feeling tears fall down my cheeks.

'Yes!' She squeals reaching out and pulling me into the scrum. 'And it could be as soon as Christmas!'

She's moving back! She's actually coming home! Happy tears drench my face, but I don't care. My best friend is returning to London!

'Alright, this calls for a celebration!' Janie cackles, jumping out of her seat and making a beeline for the bar. 'Who's for more bubbles?'

'Not me.' Eve manages, squeezing out of the fray. 'Orange juice, remember?'

'You can have more OJ when you take that damn test!' Janie scolds, rapping her knuckles on the bar.

Glancing down at the test in her hands, Eve slips through the crowd and disappears into the toilets. Finally tearing ourselves away from the happy couple, we return to our seats and revel in firing a million questions at them.

'Champagne.' The barman announces, placing a couple of icy bottles in the centre of the table and putting a stop to our conversation. 'Enjoy.'

Standing to my feet, I gather the glasses and fill each one to the brim. Once everyone has a fresh drink in their hands, I hold my fizz in the air. A buzz of adrenaline fritters around the room and I steady myself on the back of my chair.

'With all of these announcements, it only seems right that we have a toast.' I smile back at the five pairs of eyes that are staring at me expectantly. 'To Dawn, on her recent engagement. To Janie, on her new life in America...' I turn to face Li and swallow the lump in my throat. 'And to Lianna and Vernon on making the move back *home...*'

'Guys?' We spin around to see Eve standing in the middle of the bar with her t-shirt in disarray.

Sensing something is wrong, the six of us put down our glasses and rush over. With her jeans unbuttoned and a dazed expression on her face, Eve looks like she has seen a ghost. My heart pounds in my chest as she holds up the little white stick. Completely forgetting that she has peed on it, I hold it close to my face and gasp.

'Is that?' Not wanting to say it in case I am wrong, I pass it over to Gina who holds it up to the light.

'It's faint, but it's definitely there!' She gasps, handing it to Janie. 'I told you that a metallic taste was a sign of pregnancy! What did I say to you this morning? I knew it!'

Eve looks at the stick in silence and for the second time that day, my eyes fill with tears. 'I don't want to believe it.' She mumbles, clearly in shock. 'I don't dare to in case it isn't real...'

'Oh, it's there alright!' Janie hoots, waving around the stick as though it is a winning lottery ticket. 'You're for sure up the spout!'

The group bursts into hysterics, completely taking over the bar with their noise. Eve's pregnant! She's actually pregnant! I don't believe it. What are the chances? Is it luck? Is it the stone? Looking at her now, clutching the stick to her heart as she is surrounded by her friends, it doesn't matter how and it doesn't matter why. One way or another, Eve has been granted her wish and I have been granted mine.

Isn't it funny how your future can change at the drop of a hat, the booking of a plane ticket, the offer of a lifetime and the small act of peeing on a stick? What lies ahead for me? I don't really know. What I *do* know is that I can't wait to find out...

To be continued...

The Clara Andrews Series

Meet Clara Andrews
Clara Meets the Parents
Meet Clara Morgan
Clara at Christmas
Meet Baby Morgan
Clara in the Caribbean
Clara in America
Clara in the Middle
Clara's Last Christmas
Clara Bounces Back
Clara's Greek Adventure

Follow Lacey London on Twitter

@thelaceylondon

Have you read the other books in the Clara series?

Meet Clara Andrews

The fantastic first book in the bestselling Clara series by Lacey London.

The Clara series takes us on a journey through the minefields of dating, wedding-day nerves, motherhood, Barbados, America, Mykonos and beyond.

It all starts with an unfortunate first meeting…

Being young, free and single, Clara Andrews thought she had it all.

A fabulous job in the fashion industry, a buzzing social life and the world's greatest best friends are all that her heart desires. But when a chance meeting introduces her to Oliver, a devastatingly handsome American designer, Clara has her head turned.

Trying to keep the focus on her work, Clara finds her heart stolen by lavish restaurants and luxury hotels.

As things get flirty, Clara reminds herself that office relationships are against the rules. So, when a sudden memory of an evening out leads her to a gorgeous barman, she decides to see where it goes.

Clara soon finds out that dating two men isn't as easy as it seems.

Will she be able to play the field without getting played herself?

Join Clara as she finds herself landing in and out of trouble, reaffirming friendships, discovering truths and uncovering secrets.

It's time to Meet Clara Andrews… your new best friend.

Clara Meets the Parents

Grab a margarita, slip on your sunglasses and join Clara on her fun-filled trip to Mexico.

Almost a year has passed since Clara Andrews found love in the arms of delectable American Oliver Morgan, and things are starting to heat up.

The nights of tequila shots and bodycon dresses are now a distant memory, but a content Clara couldn't be happier about it.

And it's not just Clara who things have changed for...

Marc is adjusting to his new role as Baby Daddy, and Lianna is lost in the arms of the hunky Dan once again.

With her friends busy with their own lives, Clara is ecstatic when Oliver declares it time to meet the Texan in-laws.

Discovering that the introduction will take place on the sandy beaches of Mexico simply adds to her excitement, but things aren't set to be smooth sailing...

Will Clara be able to win over Oliver's audacious mother?

What secrets will unfold when she finds an ally in the beautiful and captivating Erica?

Clara is going to need a little more than sun and sand to get through this one...

Meet Clara Morgan

"How do you tell your best friend that her wedding dress is utterly vile?"

Wedding bells are ringing for Clara and Oliver in Meet Clara Morgan - the much-anticipated instalment in the Clara Andrews series.

When Clara, Lianna and Gina all find themselves engaged at the same time, it soon becomes clear that things are going to get a little crazy.

With Clara's best friends planning their own impending nuptials, it's not long before Oliver enlists the help of Janie, his feisty Texan mother, to help Clara plan the wedding of her dreams.

However, it's not long before Clara discovers that Janie's vision of the perfect wedding day is more than a little different to her own.

Will Clara be able to cope with her shameless mother-in-law?

What will happen when a groom gets cold feet?

And how will Clara handle a blast from the past who makes a reappearance in the most unexpected way possible?

Join Clara and the gang as three very different brides, plan three very different weddings.

With each one looking for the perfect fairy-tale ending, who will get their happily ever after?

Clara at Christmas

With snowflakes falling and fairy lights twinkling brightly, it can only mean one thing - Christmas shall very soon be upon us.

With just twenty-five days to go until the big day, Clara finds herself dealing with more than just the usual festive stresses.

Her plans to host the perfect Christmas Day for her American in-laws are ambushed by her BFF's clichéd meltdown at turning thirty.

With a best friend on the verge of a midlife crisis, putting Christmas dinner on the table isn't the only thing Clara has got to worry about this year.

Taking on the role of Best Friend/Therapist, Head Chef and Party Planner is much harder than Clara had anticipated.

With the clock ticking, can Clara pull things together - or will Christmas Day turn out to be the December disaster that she is so desperate to avoid?

Join Clara and the gang in this festive instalment and discover what life-changing gifts are waiting for them under the tree this year…

Meet Baby Morgan

The cot has been bought, the nursery has been decorated and a name has been chosen. All that is missing is the baby himself…

It's fair to say that pregnancy hasn't been the joyous journey that Clara had anticipated.

Extreme morning sickness, swollen ankles and crude cravings have plagued her for months, and now that she has gone over her due date, Clara is desperate to get this baby out of her.

With a lovely new home in the leafy, affluent village of Spring Oak, Clara and Oliver are ready to start this new chapter in their lives.

As Lianna is enjoying the success of her interior design firm, Periwinkle, Clara turns to the women of the village for company.

The once inseparable duo finds themselves at different points in their lives, and for the first time in Clara and Lianna's friendship, the cracks start to show.

Will motherhood turn out to be everything that Clara ever dreamed of?

Which naughty neighbour has a sizzling secret that she so desperately wants to keep hidden?

Laugh, smile and cry with Clara as she embarks on her journey to motherhood.

A journey that has some unexpected bumps along the way.

Bumps that she never expected...

Clara in the Caribbean

Pour yourself a rum punch and get ready to jet off to Barbados in this sun-soaked trip to the Caribbean.

Almost a year has floated by since Clara returned to the Big Smoke and she couldn't be happier to be back in her city.

With the perfect husband, her best friends for neighbours and a beautiful baby boy, Clara feels like every aspect of her life has finally fallen into place.

And it's not just Clara who things are going well for…

The Strokers have made the move back from the land Down Under and Lianna is on cloud nine.

Not only has Li been jetting across the globe with her interior design firm, Periwinkle, she has also met the man of her dreams… again.

For the past twelve months, Lianna has been having a long-distance relationship with Vernon Clarke - a handsome man she met a year earlier on the beautiful island of Barbados.

After spending just seven short days together, Lianna decided that Vernon was the man for her and they have been Skype smooching ever since.

Due to Li's rather disastrous dating history, it's fair to say that Clara is more than a little dubious about Vernon being 'The One'.

So, when her neighbours invite Clara to their villa in the Caribbean, she can't resist the chance of checking out the mysterious Vernon for herself.

Has Lianna finally found true love?

Will Vernon turn out to a knight in shining armour or just another fool in tin foil?

Clara in America

The Sunshine State is calling!

All aboard this drama-filled trip to sunny Florida...

With Clara struggling to find the perfect present for her baby boy's second birthday, she is pleasantly surprised when her crazy mother-in-law, Janie, sends them tickets to Orlando.

After a horrendous flight, a mix-up at the airport and a let-down with the weather, Clara begins to question their decision to fly out to America.

Despite the initial setbacks, the excitement of Orlando gets a hold of them and the Morgans start to enjoy the fabulous Sunshine State.

Too busy having fun in the Florida sun, Clara tries to ignore the nagging feeling that something isn't quite right.

Does Janie's impromptu act of kindness have a hidden agenda?

Just as things start to look up, Janie drops a bombshell that none of them saw coming.

Can Clara stop Janie from making a huge mistake, or has Oliver's audacious mother finally gone too far?

Join Clara as she gets swept up in a world of fast food, sunshine and roller coasters.

With Janie refusing to play by the rules, it looks like the Morgans are in for a bumpy ride…

Clara in the Middle

"Common sense is a flower that doesn't grow in everyone's garden…"

It's been six months since Clara's crazy mother-in-law took up residence in the Morgan's spare bedroom and things are starting to get strained.

Between bringing booty calls back to the apartment and teaching Noah curse words, Janie's behaviour has become worse than ever.

When she agreed to this temporary arrangement, Clara knew it was only a matter of time before there would be fireworks. But with Oliver seemingly oblivious to Janie's outrageous actions, Clara feels like she has nowhere to turn.

Thankfully for Clara, she has a fluffy new puppy and a job at her friend's lavish florist's to take her mind off the problems at home.

Clara finds herself feeling extremely grateful for her fabulous circle of friends, but when one of them puts her in an incredibly awkward situation, she starts to feel more alone than ever.

Will Janie's bad behaviour finally push a wedge between Clara and Oliver?

How will Clara react when Eve asks her for the biggest favour you could ever ask?

With Clara feeling like she is stuck in the middle of so many sticky situations, will she be able to keep everybody happy?

Join Clara and the gang as they tackle more family dramas, laugh until they cry, and test their friendships to the absolute limit.

Clara's Last Christmas

"Even the strongest blizzards start with a single snowflake."

Just a few months ago, life seemed pretty rosy indeed…

With Lianna back in London for good, Clara had been enjoying every second with her best friend.

From blinged-up baby shopping with Eve to wedding planning with a delirious Dawn, Clara and her friends were happier than ever.

Unfortunately, they are brought back to reality when just weeks before Christmas, Oliver and Marc discover that their jobs are in jeopardy.

With Clara helping Eve to prepare for two new arrivals, news that Suave is going into administration rocks her to the core.

It may be December, but the prospect of being jobless at Christmas means that not everyone is feeling festive.

Should they give up on Suave and move on, or can the gang work as one to rescue the company that brought them all together?

Can Clara and her friends save Suave in time for Christmas?

Jump into Clara's world for a heart-warming, hilarious ride in Clara's Last Christmas!

Clara Bounces Back

"If there were no bumps in the road, life would be an awfully dull journey..."

After taking control of Suave just six months ago, Clara and the gang are walking on sunshine. However, it's not long before the reality of owning the business starts to hit home.

With the repercussions of the Giulia Romano sex tape still hitting the company hard, Owen starts to question the stability of his investment.

Not wanting to give up on their dream, Clara and her friends have one last shot at turning things around before they throw in the towel for good.

When Marc spots a way to use the sex tape to their advantage, the gang have no choice but to put their future in the hands of Clara's brazen mother-in-law.

With a chickenpox epidemic taking over the group, Janie's outrageous persona starts to cause friction amongst Clara's group of friends.

Can they trust Janie enough to act on behalf of the company, or will her audacious behaviour be the final nail in the coffin for not only Suave, but their friendship with the Lakes?

Slip back into Clara's world and join the old gang as

they reunite in this much-anticipated continuation of the series!

Clara's Greek Adventure

"Palm trees, ocean breeze, salty air and sun-kissed hair…"

Janie, an eccentric billionaire and Mykonos.

What could possibly go wrong?

Almost a year has drifted by since Suave secured the Ianthe contract and things are going very well indeed.

With the success of the partnership shooting Suave for the stars, the gang are closer than ever and living life to the max.

Enjoying their new-found wealth proves to be a fun and exciting time for Clara and her friends, but there's one thing that's keeping a smile from Oliver's face…

After declaring their love for one another twelve months ago, Janie and Stelios have been loving life in Stelios's luxury mansion in Mykonos, but not everyone is happy for them.

Oliver has made no secret of his detest for Stelios Christopoulos, and that hatred seems to be growing stronger by the day.

However, when the gang are invited to attend Stelios's exclusive Ice Party in Mykonos, Oliver has no choice but to put his own feelings aside and represent Suave.

Will this trip give Stelios a chance to finally win over Oliver?

Is Janie's love for Stelios based on more than just fast cars and money?

With five whole days under the Greek sun awaiting them, will they all leave as friends, or will the holiday be the final straw for Oliver and his mother?

Join Clara and her friends as they jet to Mykonos and discover what Janie's heart really holds.

Have you read the other books by Lacey London?

The Anxiety Girl Series

Anxiety Girl
Anxiety Girl Falls Again
Anxiety Girl Breaks Free

Anxiety Girl

Sadie Valentine is just like you and I, or so she was...

Set in the glitzy and glamorous Cheshire village of Alderley Edge, Anxiety Girl is a story surrounding the struggles of a beautiful young lady who thought she had it all.

Once a normal-ish woman, mental illness wasn't something that Sadie really thought about, but when the three evils, anxiety, panic and depression creep into her life, Sadie wonders if she will ever see the light again.

With her best friend, Aldo, by her side, can Sadie crawl out of the impossibly dark hole and take back control of her life?

Once you have hit rock bottom, there's only one way to go...

Lacey London has spoken publicly about her own struggles with anxiety and hopes that Sadie will help other sufferers realise that there is light at the end of the tunnel.

The characters in this novel might be fictitious, but the feelings and emotions experienced are very real.

Anxiety Girl Falls Again

After an emotional voyage through the minefield of anxiety and depression, Sadie decides to use her experience with mental health to help others.

Becoming a counsellor for the support group that once helped her takes Sadie's life in a completely new direction and she soon finds herself absorbed in her new role.

Knowing that she's aiding other sufferers through their darkest days gives her the ultimate job satisfaction, but when a mysterious and troubled man attends Anxiety Anonymous, Sadie wonders if she is out of her depth.

Dealing with Aidan Wilder proves trickier than Sadie expected and it's not long before those closest to her start to express their concerns.

What led a dishevelled Aidan to the support group?

As Sadie delves further into his life, her own demons make themselves known.

Will unearthing Aidan's story cause Sadie to fall back into the dark world she fought so hard to escape?

Anxiety Girl Breaks Free

Life is full of difficult questions, but **this** shouldn't be one of them…

Aidan is back. He is standing right here in front of me. This could be the start of something special. It **should** be the start of something special. Only life isn't always that simple, is it?

With Aidan back in Cheshire and work on Blossom View well under way, it would appear that things are finally falling into place for Sadie Valentine.

Her career with the charity is keeping her busy, Aldo is enjoying being off the market and her relationship with her mother is starting to heal, but it's not long before the cracks start to show.

Not wanting to succumb to the anxiety that is slowly casting a shadow over her newly-found happiness, Sadie attempts to press on with her life regardless.

As Sadie tries to paper over the cracks, blasts from the past return to tip her world upside down in ways she could never have imagined.

With her limits being tested once again, can Sadie use her experience and strength to break free from her anxiety once and for all?

They say that the past should stay buried, but what if some ghosts simply refuse to lie low?

The Mollie McQueen Series

Mollie McQueen is NOT Getting Divorced

Mollie McQueen is NOT Having a Baby

Mollie McQueen is NOT Having Botox

Mollie McQueen is NOT Ruining Christmas

Mollie McQueen is NOT Getting Divorced

"Whoever said money can't buy happiness, obviously never paid for a divorce..."

When Mollie McQueen turned thirty, she awoke with a determination to live her best life.

Her marriage to Max was the first thing to come under scrutiny and on one sexless night in May, Mollie decided that their relationship was over.

However, when a grouchy divorce lawyer convinces Mollie there's a chance she could bow out of this life being eaten alive by a pack of cats, she starts to search for an alternative.

Opening the can of worms that is her marriage makes Mollie realise she might not be as blameless as she initially thought...

Will Mollie be able to rescue her marriage or has the lure of a life without wet towels on the bed turned her head?

One thing is for sure... Mollie McQueen is NOT getting divorced.

Mollie McQueen is NOT Having a Baby

Some women want babies, others just want to sleep like one.

Since completing their marriage counselling with therapist to the stars, Evangelina Hamilton, life in the McQueen household was looking rather cosy indeed.

Max was flying high in his new career and Mollie was finally turning her attention to renovating the house that was falling down around them.

Forming an unlikely friendship with none other than the office pariah, Timothy Slease, results in Mollie making it her mission to help him find love.

With a house to renovate and Tim's love life to sprinkle Cupid dust over, the shock of a possible pregnancy hits Mollie harder than a Ronda Rousey left hook.

Not being the type of woman who goes weak at the knees at the sight of a dirty nappy, Mollie resorts to her old coping mechanism of burying her head in the sand.

Picturing her life with a child in tow makes Mollie question everything she was previously so sure of.

With Aunt Flo refusing to play ball, house renovation

catastrophes and dating disasters might not be the only things that Mollie McQueen is expecting…

Mollie McQueen is NOT Having Botox

"Maybe she was born with it, maybe it's Botox…"

It's November. Mollie's least favourite time of the year. The days are short and the nights are cold, but when her nearest and dearest get hit with a case of the midlife crisis bug, it gives her something more than the terrible weather to complain about.

Watching her parents and in-laws putting themselves through chemical peels and hair transplants causes Mollie to make it her mission to prove that the natural approach to anti-aging is best.

Spending time with her eccentric and outlandish neighbour, Mrs Heckles, just adds to Mollie's firm opinion that growing old gracefully is the only attitude to have.

Enlisting the help of Tim's ageless girlfriend, can Mollie convince her loved ones to step away from the scalpel and learn to love the person in the mirror?

With snails, urine and some rather unorthodox tools at her disposal, Mollie certainly has a hard task on her hands, but with a troublesome cat, a huge work opportunity and a friend heading for heartache, will they all be taught a lesson in the cruellest way possible?

One thing is for sure, Mollie McQueen is NOT Having Botox.

Mollie McQueen is NOT Ruining Christmas

"Be naughty and save Santa a trip. It's better for the planet…"

There was little over a week to go until Christmas Day, but Mollie McQueen hadn't sent a single card. She hadn't purchased one gift, and she hadn't decked the halls with anything other than mountains of wet laundry.

Usually, come the first of December, the McQueen house resembled Santa's grotto. Stockings would hang from the fireplace, his and hers advent calendars would be propped up on the mantlepiece, and the two sparkly polar bears bought by Mollie's mother would stand proudly on the windowsill.

This year, all was quiet on the Christmas front. The door was missing its usual wreath, the sprig of mistletoe was absent from the hallway, and the alcove in the living room was minus the retro tree that Mollie normally insisted on rolling out on the first day of December.

When Mollie first announced her plans to strip Christmas back to basics, she received nothing but negative feedback. Max accused her of trying to ruin Christmas, Margot advised her to chuck back a daily vitamin D pill in a bid to rediscover her Christmas spirit, and Mrs Heckles had taken to singing Christmas carols through Mollie's letterbox.

Despite their grumbling, Mollie was determined to prove to everyone that you could enjoy Christmas without falling victim to the endless marketing campaigns that emotionally blackmailed you into purchasing unnecessary gifts for people who would rather have a pack of socks and a slice of Yule log.

With her no-Christmas Christmas amassing quite the guestlist, Mollie had an almighty task on her hands.

Can she convince her nearest and dearest that the true meaning of Christmas had nothing to do with expensive gifts and garish decorations?

One thing's for sure, Mollie McQueen is NOT Ruining Christmas.

Printed in Great Britain
by Amazon